Pl

$\overline{\gamma}$

HUGO AND THE BIRD

Part One

The Toothfairy

Jeff Mills

Written January 2014

authorHOUSE®

AuthorHouse™ UK
1663 Liberty Drive
Bloomington, IN 47403 USA
www.authorhouse.co.uk
Phone: 0800.197.4150

Published by AuthorHouse 01/31/2015

ISBN: 978-1-5049-3683-5 (sc)
ISBN: 978-1-5049-3682-8 (hc)
ISBN: 978-1-5049-3684-2 (e)

CONTENTS

DEDICATION

This book is dedicated to my children Patrick and Victoria

PREFACE

Jeff Mills is a dentist and lives in Devon England with his wife of over 40 years, Anne, very close to the area of Westward Ho! where the book is set.

His parents and in-laws lived in Gloucester and Glossop in Derbyshire.

On the very frequent, long car journeys to these places, his children, when young, demanded some form of "entertainment" to occupy their minds. Remember this was before in-car videos and I-Pads.

On one particular journey "Hugo" popped into his brain and thus started the saga and adventures of Hugo with his unusual friend, Bird. As the stories developed, features were incorporated taken from scenes and objects taken from the places that were being passed.

As the children grew, the demand for stories diminished until the terrible beginning of 2014 when it seemed never to stop raining. Out of sheer boredom Hugo was reborn and his adventures around his local area developed.

His involvement with the "Three Witches of Bideford" and their demise was based on the historical event that occurred in 1682 and is commemorated in a plaque on the wall of Rougemont Castle in Exeter. There was another woman Alice Molland who was accused of witchcraft and sentenced to death in 1685 but there is no record of the sentence being carried out although it probably was.

It was well recognised, even at the time, that the evidence against the witches was circumstantial and the hanging was a major miscarriage of justice but those in charge, among them a Lord North, wrote to the Secretary of State advising him to allow it to go ahead, citing, "fearing the wrath of the rabble". In view of this it was decided to go ahead, regardless.

In 2012 a group tried to organise a petition to reopen the trial of the three witches to reverse the injustice but the petition failed and the matter was dropped.

To bring the story to life the author has tried to use real places and venues and hopes that by reading the book it may give them the incentive to visit Devon and indulge themselves in one of England's most beautiful counties and even, perhaps, a Devon Cream Tea.

ACKNOWLEDGEMENTS

Many thanks to my wife, Anne, sister Jacqueline and good friend Sue for reading and constructively criticising the proof and still giving me the encouragement to complete it.

I would also like to thank my two children who, from their constant moaning on long journeys, made me come up with the ideas in the first place.

Finally I would like to thank the absolutely foul weather that started at the beginning of 2014 and made me so bored that I actually felt motivated to sit down and put pen to paper.

PROLOGUE

It was unusually cold for the time of year on the 25th of August 1682. There was a fine drizzle in the air and the thick clouds scudding across the sky made the day feel like dusk had come early.

The noise of the crowd, gathered on the green at Heavitree near Exeter in Devon in the South-West of England, suddenly ceased so that all that could be heard was the swoosh of the autumn wind in the trees surrounding the grassed area around which the curious and the ghoulish stood in eager anticipation. Even the cawing of the circling crows had stopped as they must have also sensed the magnitude of the impending event.

Slowly the hooded man moved the large handle forwards till there was a silent click followed by a load bang as the trap door shot open and the frail body of Susanna Edwards fell through the now open portal. The course rope that splayed around her thin neck snaked for a split second then, with an audible twang, tightened and the previously loose noose around Susanna's neck snapped closed.

A small cry followed by a thin gasp was all that could be heard by those still standing on the rough-hewn gallows. The legs of the unfortunate miscreant kicked and writhed in the hangman's dance for several seconds until finally, with a sickly gurgle, they went still. The rope creaked as the body slowly rotated till the bloated face of the poor victim turned toward the anticipating crowd.

Suddenly the silence was broken and the crowd erupted into an almighty roar. Men threw their hats into the air, some women screamed with ghoulish delight while others wailed with horror and hid their faces in their hands while turning away. Many, with children, sought to hide the hideous spectacle from their juvenile view but several of them wriggled out from the protective petticoats to gawp at the goings on.

Again silence was indicated by those standing on the scaffold as Mary Trembles, visibly shaking, reluctantly climbed the steps towards her inevitable fate. She constantly protested her innocence, refuting the confessions that she had made at her trial to anyone who might listen but the only response that was heard was the noise of the bolt holding the trapdoor closed sliding open, followed by the inevitable twang of the rope and the repeated uproar of the blood-thirsty rabble.

Temperance Lloyd, the eldest of the three women accused of witchcraft this day and thought to be the instigator of their supposed atrocities, calmly climbed the scaffold and looked around her as if she was out to meet friends. On reaching the top, she looked around, surveying her audience. The Sheriff of Devon asked her if she believed in Jesus Christ to which she simply replied; "Yes, and I pray Jesus Christ to pardon all my sins." The trapdoor flew open, the rope let out its final grown and thus came to an end the lives of the three witches of Bideford. The last people to be executed for witchcraft in England.

At the foot of the scaffold stood four shabbily dressed children, three girls and a young boy. Their dirty faces were streaked with the tracks of dried up tears but no tears were flowing now. All that could be seen below the dirt was a clear hated and determination for revenge on the perpetrators of this senseless miscarriage of justice on what were their parents.

CHAPTER 1

Devon

Hugo was a very active and imaginative nine year old boy, quite tall for his age and with a mane of unruly blond hair. He lived with his parents in a very old house overlooking the sea in the small North Devonshire village of Westward Ho! in the South West of England. He was proud of living here and felt a little special, as it had the unique claim to fame of being the only place in England that could boast of having an exclamation mark at the end of its name. The village was built in the late nineteenth century and named as a result of a book written by Charles Kingsley about the area and called, strangely enough, Westward Ho! It was designed and built to be a North Devon competitor for the rapidly developing holiday trade against its South Devon rival of Torquay.

His new home was a large three-storey house with small attic windows. Its southerly end was covered in rambling ivy which wrapped itself around the two small windows in the middle of the second floor. It stood out on a small headland, well away from any other building. At dusk the whole of the eastern side was cast in shadow making the house stand out like a silhouette. This had led to the locals to believe that the house was haunted and only with reluctance did they ever visit, preferring Mrs Bennett, Hugo's mother, to collect her groceries and supplies herself rather than risk having to deliver them. There were even rumours that the house but more especially the myriad of small caves and crevices in the cliff on which the house stood, was used in the past by pirates and smugglers which even further enhanced its reputation of its spookiness. Living in this house had resulted in a few strange comments from the other pupils when he had started at his new school in Abbotsham several months before but he felt they were down to jealousy streaked with a little admiration for having the bravery to stay there. It certainly made had him the topic of conversation in the first few weeks, especially amongst the girls who were unsure whether to admire his bravery or condemn his stupidity. Sometimes, at night, Hugo would lie dozing in bed counting the time between the flashes from the Hartland lighthouse that were reflected on his bedroom wall and listening to the waves crashing on the pebbles just below his bedroom window. He'd imagine the pirates and smugglers, waving their lanterns to lure unsuspecting boats onto the jagged rocks so that they could plunder the cargoes. Little was he to know what was in store for him.

Mr Bennett, Hugo's father was a dentist, a job which caused his young son some aggravation at his school. His friends, or rather fellow students, since very few were exactly friendly, seemed to take great satisfaction from reminding him that his father was locally referred to as "Butcher Bennett". A title which Hugo knew was quite unjustified as his dad took great pains to be as kind and gentle to all his patients as he could but as his father repeated frequently, "It goes with the job". He and his wife, Julia, plus Hugo and Stephanie his teenage daughter had moved to Devon only six months earlier and so, as far as Hugo was concerned, everything was still new and exciting, except school that is where he was often told off for daydreaming and lack of concentration. This sentiment was not shared by Stephanie, his thirteen, going on eighteen, year old sister. She felt that she had already explored everything that might be considered remotely interesting and was now well and truly bored and she made sure that Hugo and her parents knew about it.

The family had moved from a small red-bricked semi-detached house in a busy street in Reading. A city which, being much bigger and closer to London, had a pace of life which seemed so much faster and exciting, or that is what Stephanie kept reminding everyone at every opportunity. Her father had had the chance to buy his own dental practice in the West Country, something and somewhere he had always aspired to do. He thought that living in Devon would be like being on permanent holiday since it is renowned for its golden beaches moorland walking and warmer climate. Everyone, except Stephanie, had also thought that the move would be a great idea but before leaving Reading she had just "caught" her first boyfriend and was suffering the agonies of unrequited love plus the fact that Justin's, her little "loveykins", father was the manager of the local McDonalds and she would often get a free smoothie or snack when she met her friends there at the weekends. It was a point that had not gone unnoticed by Mrs Bennett who had become aware that Stephanie was becoming a little chubby from the regular intake of "Big Mac's and fries" and was hoping that the change of scenery might result in a change of diet. Up to now she had been right since the nearest fast food outlet was three miles away in Bideford and Stephanie was certainly losing it but in more ways than one. Withdrawal symptoms still occasionally showed themselves in noisy outbursts and tantrums often followed by days of sulking until both parents could stand it no longer and all the family were given a "treat" of a visit to McDonalds or Pizza Hut if they went over to Barnstaple, a much larger town about ten miles away. Although Hugo moaned at his sister's bad moods and tantrums he had to admit that deep down he enjoyed these visits as much as if not more than his sister. Since his father was a dentist he would insist that the family's diet was as healthy and as sugar free as possible so it was with great relish that on these occasions the rules could be broken and the burgers and fries could be washed down with a tooth-rotting Coke.

It was over a week since the last of one of these "treat" visits during the school summer holidays when Stephanie had exploded with boredom and her mother had come to her wits end. Mrs Bennett finally succumbed and drove her daughter to Barnstaple to try to make everyone calm down and clear the air with some "retail therapy". Hugo hated shopping with his mother and sister as they only ever wanted to go into Marks and Spencer's or Monsoon or other clothes shops rabbiting on about what was in fashion, or if this or that colour or style did or didn't suit them. His idea of shopping was searching through Youings the toy store at one end of the main street in Barnstaple or the computer games shop. So he told his mother that he would stay behind and find something to do at home or take Jake their golden retriever dog for a walk. After several warnings to behave himself and not to get into trouble she agreed. She and her daughter quickly changed and with a kiss and a hug from his mum for Hugo they drove off in her silver Smart car.

At first he was unsure of what to do so, while thinking, he searched through all the cupboards in the kitchen to see if he could find anything nice to eat, preferably something that was covered in chocolate or toffee, but to no avail. He did find an unopened packet of digestive biscuits but realised that opening the packet would prove his guilt so he carefully replaced them back inside the cupboard. Jake, also had seen the biscuits and wrapped himself around Hugo's legs and quietly whined hoping for a sweet treat but quickly stopped when he saw the delicacy returned to the shelf and sulked back to his bed. Hugo sighed, gave a final glance around the shelves and then decided to go for a walk with Jake along the costal path, which ran adjacent to his house, to an area called Abbotsham Cliffs. This area of the Devon coastline is fairly remote with moderately high cliff walls and was a great place to chill out as it was only accessible by walking. It, therefore, was rarely visited by the large number of holiday makers or "grockles" as the locals irreverently called them. He had only heard about this area from some of the children in his class at school which was situated in the actual village of Abbotsham, about a mile from the cliffs where he was headed. As the weather was a little overcast and blustery he donned his anorak. He did not want to join with all the "grockles" as he loved calling them, despite his mother's objection, as since he was now a resident he did not feel as if he needed to count himself in this derogatory category, a point which was always disputed by the real locals, as "a local" title was only bestowed after being a resident for over twenty five years, or longer and to some it did not apply until several generations had lived in the area. The few brave holidaymakers in the area would be huddled behind their windbreaks on Westward Ho! beach with their children digging holes in the sand and building sand castles or walking aimlessly along the sea front licking their "Hockings" ice creams. Although Hugo had only been a "resident" for six months he had already become addicted to the Hockings 99's, a cornet of ice cream with a chocolate flake pressed into the top and if he could persuade one of his parents this could be topped with some real Devonshire clotted cream. Stephanie was on a "diet" and always made herself sound a martyr by refusing the clotted cream with the result that Hugo was enforced to go without as well.

Seeing Hugo put on his coat was the trigger for Jake to get up and rush to the back door. He knew that this was a sign that the boy was going outside and Jake made sure that Hugo knew that he wanted to go as well. Hugo retrieved his old rucksack from a small cupboard, put in some snacks and a bottle of fruit juice his mother had thoughtfully left, in case he felt peckish and started on his journey. Giving his head a good rub, Hugo attached a lead to Jake's collar and opened the back door. The eager dog jumped forward almost pulling Hugo over but after locking the door they both turned and headed out of the garden and onto the coastal path. The track they were walking on was in fact the bed of the old railway line that used to run between Westward Ho! and Bideford. Unfortunately the train journey had been very slow and was soon superseded by a road which proved faster leaving the railway obsolete. The lines had been torn up and now all that remained was the track bed. Fortunately parts of it had been gritted which made walking and cycling on it much easier.

The tide was on the way out and so Hugo knew that by the time he reached the cliffs at Abbotsham he would still have plenty of time to explore around the beach before it started to come back in again. It was always exciting, beachcombing at low water, as you never knew what you might find that had been washed overboard from a passing ship or even a wreck, as this part of the Devonshire coastline was inundated with the underwater rotting hulls of the boats that had foundered on its ragged and jagged coastline. His mother had stressed the dangers of getting caught by the tide on many occasions and it was not uncommon to see reports in the local newspaper about holidaymakers having to be rescued by the local air sea rescue helicopter based across the estuary at Chivenor. It had passed through his mind that it would be extremely exciting to be rescued in this way and get a ride in a helicopter as well. He was sure that it would make all his schoolmates really jealous when he returned for the autumn term, though he would have to pretend that he was very sorry and contrite for having caused such a fuss. However, he knew that such an act of apparent irresponsibility would result in very serious repercussions from his parents especially his dad and so he quickly dismissed the idea.

As he walked along, jumping and side walking every now and then to dodge the puddles that lay along the track, Jake, his retriever and constant companion on these "adventures" suddenly jumped forward, pulling the lead out of Hugo's hand, and bounded off in pursuit of a very lively rabbit that could be seen about a hundred meters ahead. Despite Hugo's frantic calls and whistles for him to come back, Jake kept up the chase and soon disappeared over the crest of a small hill.

The coastal path was bounded on the landward side by a barbed-wire fence which Hugo knew was not only designed to keep animals off the path but also to stop people trespassing onto the farmland. He was even more concerned that there were sheep and other animals in the fields and he had heard tales where farmers had shot stray dogs that had ventured onto their land worrying and even killing some sheep. The thought of Jake being shot filled Hugo with dread and so, despite his natural instinct to stay on the path and keep out of trouble he found a section of fence, where possibly badgers had scrapped a large gully, and wriggled himself under it. As he stood up he heard a loud tear and looking down found that he had caught his trousers on one of the barbs on the fence and torn a long slit on the right side. He knew that this would certainly land him in some trouble when he returned home but the thought of Jake lying in a pool of blood with a bullet in him spurred him on.

He had just crested a small hill when he saw Jake, half buried, with his head down a large hole, presumably the bolt hole of the rabbit he was chasing. His tail was beating enthusiastically back and forth while his front legs were frantically pawing at the margins of the burrow in an effort to enlarge it so that his quarry could be traced and caught. Hugo called and pulled at Jake's collar to try to withdraw him from the hole and it was several minutes before both dog and he finally fell backwards into heap of flailing arms, legs and tail. It was when Hugo started to stand up that he heard another loud tear and low and behold he had fallen on an old bramble branch which had become entangled in his trousers and there was now another large split to match the one on the other side.

Hugo knew that now he'd be in real trouble when he returned home and was seriously contemplating the consequences and planning his excuses when he noticed a large elongated rock with a strange zigzag pattern lying in the entrance of the burrow. He did not want Jake to escape again and get him into even more trouble so having securely refastened the lead back onto Jake's collar he grabbed the stone, brushed off the dust and mud and then with no more than a further cursory glance threw it into his rucksack. He was careful not to crush the bottle of fruit juice he had packed together with a fruit crunchy bar and a banana which he now noticed was rather squashed after his backward fall from extricating Jake from the rabbit hole. He also avoided smashing the doggy chew and bottle of water wrapped in a polythene bag, for use in case of a doggy emergency, which he always remembered whenever he and Jake went out together. Hugo picked up his rucksack and fitted it back over his shoulders. He was amazed how heavy it now seemed but never gave it a second thought and decided that rather head on to Abbotsham Cliffs he would turn back and get home before his mother returned home from her shopping trip. That way he could change his trousers and put the torn ones in the wash basket so that when his mother came to wash and iron them she would think that they had become entangled in the washing machine or something and it was that that had torn them.

Jake was very fretful all the way home and kept barking and jumping up at Hugo's rucksack, even after Hugo stopped to give him his doggy chew, a drink of water and use the polythene bag to pick up Jake's waste, something Hugo hated doing. By the time he stepped back into his house he was quite exhausted and glad to tie Jake onto the long lead attached to his kennel and take off the now extremely heavy rucksack. He rushed up to his room eased his arms through the straps of his burden and threw it onto his bed where it bounced a few times and then lay still. He was sure that he had heard a faint moan as the rucksack hit the bed but paid no attention to it. He wearily went downstairs into the kitchen and made himself a jam sandwich washed down by a glass of orange squash.

Within minutes Hugo felt recovered from his expedition. He bounded upstairs and returned to his room. He took off his muddy and torn trousers and extracted a clean pair of jeans out of his bedroom cabinet drawer. Putting them on, he quickly rushed down to the laundry room and carefully hid the torn pair towards the bottom of the pile of washing so that they would less likely be noticed and delay the inevitable. He just made it. As he left the laundry room he heard his mother's Smart car draw up onto the gravel drive. He suddenly had a brainwave. He noiselessly sneaked out of the back door grabbing Jake's lead as he went. He then crept to the dogs kennel and quietly clipped the lead onto his collar. The dog looked a little puzzled as he knew that he had had his walk and was now quite happy sprawled out, belly up in the sunshine which had now come out. Hugo coaxed Jake up and inched round the house. Slowly they skirted the house until Hugo and Jake were on the track that went to and from Abbotsham Cliffs. He then raised himself to his full height and shouted a cheery "Hello!" to his mother. He then ran up to his mum and gave her a big hug but making sure that she saw from which direction he had come and that he had on spotless, untorn trousers.

He retied Jake to his kennel and helped his mother empty her car of shopping, taking the groceries into the kitchen. He glowered at Stephanie who was still standing by the car making cooing noises into her mobile phone. In return she put her thumb to her nose and wiggled her fingers. Hugo was keen to see if his mother had bought him any special treats and with relief he noticed that she had a pack of jam doughnuts strategically placed on the top of her bag. She noticed Hugo eying the illicit goodies and smiling gave him permission to take one. He needed no second asking and hungrily tore open the pack and pulled out the largest sugar- coated doughnut he could see. Smirking as he walked past Stephanie he took his sticky prize up to his room licking some of the sugar from the outside as he went.

He was keen to examine the stone which he had prised from the entrance of the rabbit hole and which, whether he imagined it or not, had seemed to get heavier as he carried it back home. He put down the doughnut on a piece of paper on his bedside table and seizing his rucksack by the bottom he shook out all its treasures onto the floor. In addition to the large stone, the fruit juice and snacks, which in all the excitement he had forgotten about, there also tumbled out a dirty bunch of tissues, a half- finished tube of fruit gums, which he had managed to slip past his father, one pound and sixty three pence in loose change, which he had taken to buy some more sweets or an ice cream while his parents weren't watching, and a small penknife which he had to be sure that he did not accidentally take to school during term time as he would certainly end up in trouble as well as it being confiscated. The penknife was one of his most treasured possessions and had been given to him, without his parent's knowledge, by his granddad. The penknife had a red handle with a small cross emblem embedded in it. His granddad had said it was a Swiss Army knife which made Hugo feel very grown up as its owner. It had a small sharp blade, a bottle opener, a screwdriver and a pair of scissors. At the ends of the handle was a small pair of tweezers and a tooth pick which if his father ever caught him with the knife he could use as an excuse for its possession since he could say he used it to keep his teeth clean. This had been his granddad's idea though Hugo thought that was also the excuse that his granddad would give if he was accused of being stupid and giving him a "dangerous" play thing.

Hugo enjoyed being with his grandparents as they spoilt him so much when his parents weren't there. Even Stephanie was almost human even friendly when staying with them but I suspect that they gave in to her every whim to avoid the sulks and tantrums she fell into whenever her parents were around. Unfortunately, since their move from Reading, Hugo had seen little of his grandparents. They had come down to Devon when his parents first moved into their new house to give a hand and babysit the children while it was redecorated and refurnished. It was possibly the best fortnight that he could remember. Everything was new and exciting; the weather was cold but sunny so that Hugo, Stephanie and their grandparents could explore the coast and moors. They even hired bicycles and went for a ride along the "Tarka Trail", part of the walking and cycling trail that follows the old track bed of the railway that went from Bideford to Great Torrington and beyond. They stopped at the Puffing Billy, which once was actually Great Torrington railway station but is now a pub. Granddad liked to stop here for a drink and a snack. He said it gave a purpose for the journey. The children both liked it too as they were each bought large glasses of Coke and a bag of sweets, "To give you the energy for the homeward trip." Granddad said with a smile on his face. Stephanie moaned when it was time to leave the pub, insisting that she was tired. Fortunately granddad found a length of old rope in the ditch and used it to tie Stephanie's bike to the back of his so that he could tow her along without any effort on her part. Hugo fumed when he saw her secretly smirking as they hurtled past him on the way home.

The fortnight of their visit disappeared so quickly and his grand- parents had only returned for a flying visit once since then. Still, grandma had made and brought with her some really stodgy puddings and a big fruit cake which Hugo's father said were very unhealthy and tooth rotting but everyone noticed he had the biggest pieces of all.

As the winter and early spring were left behind the longer days and warmer weather had allowed Hugo to become more familiar with his new surroundings and the local characters that lived close by. It was while his mother was talking to the local butcher that he first heard about the strange happenings that had occurred in the area all seemingly to centre around the house where they were now living, though he did notice that after telling these tails the butcher would wink at my mother and touch his nose. These stories were further embellished and exaggerated by the children at his school who delighted in warning him that he was going to meet some horrible fate, however this made Hugo feel special and rather than be frightened he felt it gave him a sense of bravery in that he was able to live with this constant threat.

Hugo was about to pick up and sink his teeth into the delicacy lying on his bedside table when his mother called for him to come down for his lunch, so he carefully placed the cake onto the table by his bed and went downstairs where his mother had already prepared a salad followed by a rhubarb yogurt. This was not Hugo's idea of lunch but the promise of the doughnut upstairs made him eat it without complaint. Meanwhile, in Hugo's bedroom the strange round rock with the zigzag pattern lay on the bed soaking in the sunshine and slowly becoming warmer.

CHAPTER 2

What Lies Beneath?

The smell was terrible, like a mixture of overcooked Brussels sprouts, old ash trays and smelly socks but this did not seem to bother the tall, stick-thin shadowy figure that bent over some small glass tubes. An immense copper still stood in the corner and issued a dense haze of yellow-green fumes which almost enveloped it. A thick oily blood-red liquid oozed from a thin spout at the bottom. The air was filled with a deep noisy gurgling which rose above some small pathetic whimpers but from exactly where or what was causing them it was impossible to see. The whole of the rear wall of the large cavern was taken up by the enormous shadow of what at first glances might be mistaken for a cat but on closer examination did not resemble in any shape or form that warm cuddly pet that would not look out of place in front of a roaring fire.

The animal, or whatever it called itself, was not as big as first thought as it was sat in front of a smoky oil lamp that was projecting its shadow onto the wall making it look larger than it really was. Nevertheless, it looked like a cross between a leopard and a sabre-toothed tiger with the spots and body size of the leopard but the head and fags of the sabre-toothed tiger. It roused itself and padded noiselessly back and forth across the floor, never taking its bright green eyes off the figure working at the still. Yet the animal was not the source of the whimpering. In the dim light from the flickering lamp could just be seen a small alcove in which was stacked several old, splintered wooden boxes. It was from within these boxes that there emanated the sorrowful sounds underlying the gurgle of the still.

The cloaked figure moved silently around the table engrossed in her work till finally she coughed, spat on the floor and slowly pulled down the hood from over her head revealing a gaunt and wizened face, partially obscured by thin lank locks of greasy grey-brown hair. Her eyes were sunk so much into their sockets that had it not been for the creased grey-white mottled skin that hung limply over her face you would think that it was a living skull. However, the most noticeable feature was a thick red scar that ran, as far as could be seen, round her neck and the hollow socket where one of her eyes had been. "There now my pretty" she whispered to the stalking animal. "The mixture is ready. All we need now is some lucky victim to try it out on. Who shall it be?" The figure turned and looked down at the animal, who, despite appearing to be quite able to tear the figure apart with one slash of its large fangs, whimpered and backed away, fully understanding the figures thoughts and the possibilities that might lie ahead.

"Don't worry my pretty" she cackled, "It won't be you - this time. No! For this little potion I need something or someone special to try it out on." At this she turned with a flourish of her cloak and gazed menacingly at the wooden boxes from where the moaning had come. Immediately the moaning suddenly changed to a cacophony of high pitched screams and the boxes started to shake and rattle as the poor creatures encaged within fought desperately to escape anticipating what was to come.

As the figure slowly ambled over to the boxes the screaming intensified to the point that the whole of the cave seemed to resonate with the sound. The old hag pushed and moved the boxes with her old and dirty boot until she found one at the back which did not move and from which no sound was heard to come. "Ah my beauty you're just what I need." she said to no one in particular and stooping down she lifted the box from the floor, turned and walked back to her workbench, whereupon she shook the box vigorously and dropped it onto the table.

From within the box was heard a small voice which shouted "Careful you clumsy old hag I was trying to get some sleep."

"Oh you'll have plenty of time for that." gloated the figure and slowly, with great care, she opened the lid of the box, inserted her scrawny hand and pulled out a small figure of what looked like a tiny man. He was about twenty centimeters tall with a bright blue coat, vivid yellow trousers and a big floppy red hat. He had large rosy cheeks and somewhat large nose.

"Hello again, you old hag," the small man shouted. "I see that you're still as ugly as ever. It's about time you made one of your potions to make you look a little less grotesque."

"I'll soon fix your cheek." snarled the cloaked figure, and with that she took from a drawer a long piece of string and started to wind it around the arms and legs of the small man. However, in the dim light the little man had managed to pick up a piece of wood from his box and instead of the figure winding the string around his legs she was in fact winding it round the wood. When she had finished she turned and left the man on the table while she went over to the still to retrieve one of the small glass jars that held the blood-red potion that she had been brewing.

This was the opportunity that the little man had been waiting for and quickly and quietly releasing himself from the string bonds he ran along the bench and using the handle of an old sweeping brush that was propped against the table he slid down onto the floor.

When the figure turned round with the jar in her hand and saw that the little man had escaped she screamed with fury and in blind temper dashed the glass jar onto the floor. There was a loud explosion and the large cat-like animal screeched and jumped high into the air knocking over several more jars of various descriptions which either exploded themselves or gave off clouds of rancid-smelling smoke and steam.

The figure ran around the cave screaming obscenities and kicking over buckets and jars to get to the little man who himself was doing his best not to get entangled in the mess of thick ooze on the floor and the debris from the exploding jars. The figure screamed at the animal "Snatch! Get over here and kill this dratted gnome." Snatch emerged from the corner of the cave where he had been cowering but showed no enthusiasm to rush around the puddles of potions and broken glass to fulfil his owner's demands. Instead it gingerly crept around the outside of the walls avoiding the mess and the anger of the now hysterical figure who was charging wildly around the cave waving the broom that the little gnome had used to climb down off the table.

In all the commotion the gnome had silently worked his way around the walls of the cave until he found himself at the door that led to the entrance of the tunnel that led to the outside and freedom. Fortunately, he was able to squeeze under the bottom of the door close to the hinge where some of the wood had rotted away. He knew that if he could make it up the tunnel there would be daylight at the end and safety, for Kadavera, the witch, as that was her name, would never move out into sunlight for its rays were her only weakness. If she ever ventured out into sunshine she would die.

CHAPTER 3

The Bird

Hugo's mother was blissfully unaware of the trick that he had played on her to avoid her finding out about his torn trousers and without too much attention had thrown the pile of dirty washing into the washing machine. His father had come home early as his last patient had cancelled and since it had now turned out to be a warm sunny evening all the family were out on the lawn enjoying a barbeque. Stephanie was being on her best behaviour as Hugo's mother had also invited her friend Mrs Edmunds, who just happened to be the mother of Stephanie's new boyfriend, "Martykins" as Hugo had heard her call him on her mobile phone.

Hugo did not think much of Martin, his real name. He was much taller than Hugo, just turned fifteen but with terrible greasy hair and acne. On the few occasions that Martin had deigned to speak to Hugo, whatever Hugo had done Martin had done it, but better or for longer which Hugo knew was him just bragging to impress Stephanie, he always spoke down to him as if he was much younger than he was. However, Hugo was delighted when Mrs Edmunds let slip during the barbeque that Martin was terrified of spiders. This gem of information would surely come in useful at some time in the future he thought to himself.

Just then, almost as if it were planned, while Hugo's father was dishing up the burgers and sausages onto the table from the barbeque, a spider, alright it was a fairly large one about three centimetres across, fell from an overhanging tree branch onto the dining table about a centimetre from where Martin had his hand to grab a burger. Without warning Martin jumped up from the table with an almighty scream that would have done any girl proud. His chair went flying backwards and in his panic he had grabbed the table cloth and almost like a conjuror pulled it from beneath all the plates and dining wear, with the exception that conjurors leave all the crocks standing. Martin didn't. The plates crashed to the floor, the milk and fruit juice jug upended, spilling all their contents over Hugo's mother and Mrs Edmunds. In an effort to stop everything else spilling over Hugo's father made a grab for the tea pot and in doing so lost his grip on the plate of freshly cooked burgers and sausages he was bringing from the barbeque, sending them sailing into the air so that they landed in disarray in the flower bed and over the lawn. Jake did not need an invitation to partake in this abundant out-pouring of food and before anyone had noticed he had wolfed down two beef burgers and was on his second sausage.

Martin and his mother were distraught with embarrassment. Had it not been for Stephanie holding and consoling Martin he would have burst into tears. Everyone else was intrigued to know what was wrong as they had not seen the spider and it was only after Mrs Edmunds had finished apologising profusely that she was able to explain about Martin's phobia. Hugo's mother and father were most sympathetic despite realising that the whole dinner was now beyond the point of no return. Hugo was convinced that he saw then both snigger when their backs were turned. Only Jake seemed to be enjoying the situation. He was now on his forth burger.

With the dinner in tatters and irretrievable, Hugo's father suggested that they all go inside and he would pop down to the nearby chip shop and get fish and chips for everyone. This idea was met with whole-hearted approval so that, while everyone except Hugo's mother, who busied herself tidying up the mess and Jake who was still gorging on the unexpected bonanza of food, moved into the lounge in the house, Hugo's father took his car, a silver Volvo V70, and went to get the fish and chips while Hugo himself spent the rest of the evening smiling and trying to re-enact the event in his own mind.

That day the weather had changed from being overcast when Hugo started his walk to Abbotsham Cliffs to warm bright sunshine which had streamed into Hugo's bedroom facing the sea. The zigzag rock had lain on the floor beside Hugo's bed getting steadily warmer. Small vibrations started to appear and the rock started to perceptively move. At the start the movements were intermittent and hardly noticeable but slowly and surely they increased in length and amplitude. Before long the stone was spinning round and round and a distinct tapping could be heard coming from the inside. A small crack started to appear along one side of the stone.

It was at this point that Hugo came into his room to get some foreign stamps to show Martin, who he was sure would already have them plus countless others of the set. The stone had moved around so much that it now rested just in front of the door to Hugo's bedroom so that on entering Hugo tripped over the stone and fell headlong onto his bed. Without thinking he picked himself up grabbed the stone and threw it onto the top of his toy cupboard. With a little effort and pulling out half the contents of the cupboard he found his quarry, he seized his stamp album and ran back down the stairs to the lounge where amid the now rolled up empty fish and chip papers he proudly displayed his not inconsiderable stamp collection to Martin and his mother. Hugo finally found and opened the page where lay his pride and joy, a triangular collection from Mongolia issued in 1984 depicting a series of rodents. He knew that they were not particularly valuable but this was a mint set and were very pretty and colourful and he loved them. Martin's mother glanced across and said loudly, "Oh don't you have some like that Marty dear?" Martin smirked, "Oh yes but mine are from the Cape of Good Hope and are much more valuable than those." With this he turned to Stephanie and grinned with a sort of snooty flick to his head. Stephanie smiled back with drooling eyes that made Hugo feel positively sick.

Hugo decided that he could not stand the present company anymore and so slamming his stamp album shut, which made his mother give him a very disapproving look, he gave a false yawn and announced that his walk earlier in the day had worn him out and he was going to his room for an early night. Mr and Mrs Bennett looked at each other in absolute amazement. It was unheard of for Hugo to "have an early night" in fact it was quite the opposite as he always needed ordering to go to bed. Still his parents smiled at each other at their good fortune at not having to go through the nightly performance of shouting at him to "get up those stairs. Immediately!" and having kissed him good night, which embarrassed Hugo having Martin see him being kissed by his mother, he politely turned to Mrs Edmunds, wished her good night, then deliberately avoiding Martin and his sister's stare he left the room and climbed dejectedly up the stairs to his bedroom. As he went he muttered under his breath, "Oh mine are much more valuable than those!" "You wait," he thought to himself. "I'll show him. Stupid show off!" With that he kicked open his bedroom door, shuffled inside and slammed the door behind him. He tossed his album back into the cupboard with little reverence as Martins snide remarks had seemingly devalued it and threw himself onto his bed with his feet hanging over the side.

The force of the album hitting the cupboard dislodged the zigzag stone that Hugo had picked up earlier and it fell off the top of the cupboard and onto the floor, whereupon it rolled and stopped at Hugo's feet. Hugo sat up from his bed and looked down wondering what had touched his toes. It was only now that he remembered the stone. This was the first time that he had had to really study the stone as, since he had picked it up it, he had not given it much thought or attention. Bending down he reached out his hand to pick it up but was amazed to feel that it was now so warm that he could not touch it comfortably and also that it seemed to be vibrating. He jumped off his bed and, grabbing a towel from the end of his bed he wrapped the stone it and lifted it onto his bed to study it more closely.

All movement suddenly stopped from the stone for about a minute then it started to vibrate again and sort of buzz. Hugo was about to rush down to tell his parents what he had found and what was happening to it when he remembered that Martin and his mother were still downstairs and he did not want to appear a fool if the rock turned out to be just a "rock". While Hugo wandered in indecision on what to do there was a small screeching noise, like someone's nails scraping down a blackboard and the top of the stone flew off, narrowly missing the window of Hugo's bedroom, and slowly a strange animal appeared to emerge from inside.

At first, all Hugo could see was a streak of bright purple running down what appeared to be a neck. As he became immobilised with amazement the animal inside the stone started to move in an effort to extricate itself from its remains. The bright purple streak slowly moved back and forth till suddenly it flicked out of the stone and a large head appeared. The head was similar to that of an ostrich which at first glances made Hugo think that that was what it was but this head had large ears which were now unfolding. Before Hugo could register his surprise the neck extended and the purple streak became larger as the body of the weird looking animal slowly wiggled and pushed its way out of the remains of the stone.

As the animal slowly worked is way out and it's, somewhat large size became more and more apparent Hugo started to feel a little nervous and started to back away from the emerging creature. He wanted to call for his parents but somehow he seemed rooted to the spot and could not move or speak. His eyes had become fixated on the scene emerging before him.

With sudden pop and bang the last part of the animal wiggled out of the stone, the remains of which fell loudly onto the floor. Hugo heard a scraping from downstairs and a door opening and Mrs Bennett was heard to call up the stairs to ask if everything was alright. Hugo was about to shout out that everything was certainly not alright when the weird animal quickly turned and in a voice identical to Hugo's shouted, "Everything's OK mum."

Hugo fell back in absolute surprise but the Bird, for now that it had fully emerged from the stone was unsteadily trying to stand. I was now becoming fairly obvious that it was what is was. It stretched its long neck and shook, ruffling its wings and feathers. It nearly knocked Hugo off the bed when it started to flap its wings which seemed to stretch the whole width of the bedroom. The bird continued ruffling, stretching and preening for at least two minutes when it suddenly became aware of Hugo who was half off and half on his bed and gripping the duvet for stability and protection. The bird gave a sort of cough and squawk turned its head to look directly at Hugo and said in a low crackly almost foreign accent. "Hello young man. Who are you?"

This was the last thing that Hugo had expected and this time he really did fall off the bed and banged his head on the leg of a chair that was standing in the corner. Or was standing, for now it fell down with a crash. It was a moment after that Mrs Bennett's voice again came up the stairs asking if everything was alright. As before the bird replied in Hugo's voice that everything was alright and that he had accidentally knocked over a chair. When Hugo heard the sound of the lounge door being closed he raised himself off the floor and with trepidation and somewhat shaky voice said to the animal. "Whwhwho are you and whwhwhat are you?"

"Oh let me introduce myself" said the bird "I am an Ostricoelefantasaurus, but people usually just call me Bird."

"Ostriwhaticus?" said Hugo.

"Well to give you my full name it is Ostricoelefantidae Philatitrocusfumaritor Minor".

"Minor?" questioned Hugo.

"Oh yes" said Bird "my cousin Ostricoelefantasaurus Major lives the other side of the world in Tasmania but I must admit that I have not heard from him for a long time. Of course he's much bigger than me and can make himself look like a small hill so even if you looked straight at him you would not realise that he was there. This may be why no one ever mentions seeing him."

"But how is it you can talk and talk in English and sound like me especially straight from a stone?" Bird was about to reply when it noticed the doughnut on the floor from where it had fallen when the table had been knocked over when Hugo had fallen from the bed. Without asking, it seized the treat plus the other food items on the floor and in one movement ate the lot, wrappers and all. Hugo froze and just looked on in disbelief as his anticipated late night supper disappeared before his eyes.

Bird licked his beak and looked around to see if there was anything else edible but seeing nothing sat down on its haunches and began

"Well it's a long story." replied Bird," but it's like this;"

CHAPTER 4

The Witches of Bideford

Many years ago in July 1682 a local woman, living in the then thriving port of Bideford situated along the river Torridge on the North Devon coast was found to be ill. Her name was Grace Thomas and her sickness was thought to have been brought on by witchcraft. A local well respected shopkeeper, called Thomas Eastchurch, Grace's brother in law, claimed that Temperance Lloyd, another old woman living in the area had used witchcraft to cause the injuries to her. Other people joined in the accusations saying that they had seen a cat and a magpie enter Temperance's house, which were all signs of the devil. They all accused her of witchcraft together with two other associates of Temperance, Mary Trembles and Susanna Edwards. Grace Thomas was found to have nine pricks in her knee and Temperance Lloyd admitted piercing a piece of leather nine times which confirmed her guilt. Thomas Eastchurch had said that he had overheard Temperance Lloyd confess to meeting "something in the likeness of a black man" who had tempted her to go and torment Grace Thomas.

The three old women were arrested and locked up in the old chapel that stood at the end of the bridge over the river Torridge in Bideford. There they remained for several days before being taken to the local justices, Thomas Gist, Mayor of Bideford, and John Davie, Alderman. Here the justices heard evidence from several other people who accused the women of seeing signs and overhearing talk of many acts of witchcraft. As a result the three women were committed to trial at Exeter assizes.

At the women's trial, when questioned by the rector Michael Ogilby, Temperance Lloyd confessed to turning into a cat, stealing a doll and placing it in Grace Thomas's bedchamber but she denied using any magic to inflict the illness. Later, however, she admitted to all the charges against her as well as killing William Herbert, Lydia Burman and Anne Fellow. She also admitted to blinding Jane Dallyn in one eye, however, these admissions were made as she believed that she was still under the protection of the black man.

The other two women were similarly accused of causing illness to other people and being an associate of Temperance Lloyd. Much of the evidence against the two women came from statements of Joan Jones and William Edwards who both claimed that they had overheard

Susanna Edwards confessing that she had intimate relations with the Devil. Mary Trembles similarly confessed but said that she was forced into it by Susanna Edwards.

Despite most of the evidence being unsubstantiated and hearsay all three women were found guilty and sentenced to be hung. At exactly three o'clock on Thursday August 25th 1682 the sentence was duly carried out at Heavitree just outside Exeter.

Several years prior to these fateful events Mary Trembles had lived with her two small daughters, Jane and Anne, in a small hovel on the far bank of the river Torridge in an area now known as "East the Water". Her neighbour, Susanna Edwards, also had a small daughter, Mary and the orphaned son of her brother. The son, called Stephen, was much younger than the three girls but all four were the greatest of friends and were inseparable as they all played together. Their respective fathers had all been drowned while working as fishermen out of Bideford harbour. To all intent they were one big family and Stephen regarded the girls as sisters.

Although living in a very poor part of Bideford the women had developed a great reputation as healers and it was not uncommon to see both rich and poor come to the house for remedies to help cure the ailments prevalent at that time. These skills they also passed on to the children especially Stephen who, though being very young, seemed to have a natural ability to learn the skills which the women practiced. The local people often used to refer to the family as the "White witches of Bideford".

Everyone was as happy as could be expected under constant strain of being poor until one day, a middle-aged women, called Grace Thomas, came to see Mary Trembles to see if she could charm some warts off her fingers. While at the house, Temperance Lloyd, a friend of Susanna Edwards came to visit. Temperance was owed a small amount of money by Grace and on seeing her there asked for it to be repaid. An argument ensued and Grace Thomas stormed out of the house vowing to get even with "You stupid old hags". Thus started the train of events that would lead to the deaths of the children's parents and friend.

The years ticked by after the hanging during which the children grew into adulthood. Rarely were they as cheerful as they were before the terrible murders, as they considered the deaths of the three women to be a major miscarriage of justice. All four continued to practice and develop the skills that their mothers had shown them but with an increased vigour and a strong longing to redress the injustice that had been done.

Fifteen years later in 1697 a new judge, Sir Thomas Raymond, came to Bideford with his son and daughter. He was a rather bossy and dominating type of person and rapidly became very disliked as did his children who thought that they were better than everyone else.

One day the judge and his children returned to Bideford from Exeter, after overseeing the hanging of a criminal that had been caught stealing bread for his family and sentenced to death, his children became ill and were on the point of dying. The judge was at his wits end as he really loved his children despite them being so obnoxious to everyone else. He insisted on the best doctors in the area to come to try and treat his children but they could do nothing until a servant suggested that he consult Mary Edwards the now local healer.

He ordered the servant to run immediately to the house where she and her friends lived and under pain of death insist that they attend the sick children. When the servant reached the house he found it empty as all the family had gone to help a fisherman in Appledore, a small fishing village a few miles from Bideford, downriver, where one of the fisherman's sons had fallen into the river Torridge and nearly drowned. The servant knew that if he did not return with the healer that the judge would take his anger out on him so he commandeered a cart and drove as fast as he could to Appledore, seeking Mary Edwards.

It was late in the evening when he eventually found her but she said that she could not come as the life of the fisherman's son was held in the balance but instead Anne, Jane and Stephen would return with him. By the time that the cart pulled up to the house of the judge it was very late and the whole of Bideford was in total darkness except for the flickering glow of candles illuminating the dim interiors of the houses. There was no moon to be seen and the wind was beginning to pick up. A storm was on its way. On entering the house they found the judge in a terrible rage, demanding why they had taken so long to come and didn't they know who he was and how important and better his children were over some pathetic fisherman's son and why hadn't Mary Edwards come instead of sending these "second raters". Despite all the animosity the three went to the bedsides of the judges ailing offspring. It was obvious that the two sick children were in a very bad way and Stephan told the judge that it did not look very hopeful and to prepare himself for the worse.

At this the judge flew into the most violent rage that his servants had ever seen and taking him by the throat, swore to Stephen that if his children died then so will he. Calmly Stephen turned and returned to the room with the sick children. He and the two sisters worked tirelessly through the night and most of the next day without sleep and very little food or water but it was hopeless and as the church bell tolled ten in the evening, both the son and the daughter of the judge died.

Out of grief, frustration and anger on hearing the news the judge picked up a large walking cane and began to lay into Stephen who had jumped in front of the women to try and protect them from the blows. The attack never seemed to stop until the judge stood panting and Stephen lay broken in a pool of blood on the floor of the children's room.

It was several minutes before the judge regained some semblance of composure. Everyone around, the servants and the sisters were struck dumb with shock until finally a small servant girl started to scream which in turn was echoed by the sisters and other servants. It was obvious that, now he was beginning to calm down, the repercussions of what he had just done were rapidly going through the judge's brain and the accusation and punishment for murder that would befall him. Without further ado he shouted to his servants, "Arrest those witches! They've just killed my children."

The servants were still in shock but also very fearful and intimidated by the overbearing judge. No one was prepared to argue with him having previously seen the beatings and on one occasion the imprisonment of anyone who dared stand up against him. He ordered two of his biggest servants to pick up the body of Stephen and throw it in the river. The impending storm will wash it out to sea and even if it is found people will think it is the body of a shipwrecked sailor or a fisherman that's fallen overboard, he thought to himself. "And get that bloody mess off my floor!" he shouted to a white and trembling servant girl who seemed rooted to the spot with terror. Slowly the servants started to move. The two big ones lifted the still blood-dripping body of Stephen onto one of the sheets off the dead children's bed and wrapped it around him. Hoisting the corpse onto their shoulders they manoeuvred their burden through the door and out into the night. The other male servant tentatively bunched up the sobbing and distraught sisters and ushered them out of the room and down a dark corridor and into a small cupboard which he opened, pushed them inside, then shut the door and turned the big iron key in the lock. The judge went to his room to plan his next move.

The next day he gathered his servants together and with the promise of double pay that week, convinced them all that his version of events was correct and whatever was said by the two women was a pack of lies. It was a little while after this meeting that he remembered that the friends also lived with another witch. He decided to refer to them like this so that the public, when they heard about the events of that night, would be on his side as witchcraft was still feared at that time.

Since he had taken swift action, news about the attack had not yet become generally known so he decided to send his servant back to Appledore to get the third witch to come to him warning him not to breathe a word to her of what had happened.

At the fisherman's cottage the young son of the fisherman had responded well to the potions and herbs that Mary had ministered to him and was now feeling much better, much to the relief of his parents. She was just sitting down to a bowl of soup and a wedge of bread that the fisherman's wife had made for her when the judge's servant coyly knocked on the door. He explained to her that her friends needed her quickly and that she must return with him forthwith. Thus it was mid- afternoon when she entered the judges house.

Immediately, he ordered his servants to arrest her and lock her up with other two witches. Reluctantly they obeyed and through the shouts and protestations she was bundled down the corridor and thrown into the cupboard with her still sobbing friends. Through the sobs and tears the two women explained to Mary the events of the night before and the sad, violent end that had befallen Stephen.

Several weeks went by during which they were taken in chains from the dingy cupboard to and even dingier prison cell at the notorious prison near Exeter in Devon where 15 years earlier their mothers had been brutally sentenced to death. A trial was set and took place but the verdict was a forgone conclusion as the judge had bribed all the jurors and witnesses for the defence and public opinion had been raised to fever pitch proclaiming the women as witches. It did not take long before the presiding judge, a Roger North, son of the original judge in their mothers trial and similarly named, who, by chance, happened to be a great friend of Sir Thomas Raymond, placed the black cap on his head and sentenced the three women to death by hanging for the crime of witchcraft. The three witches, as he referred to them. were taken down to await execution "which must be done without delay." he insisted, "to avoid inflaming the rabble." Thus, two days later, with no time given for an appeal, at three o'clock on the 25th August 1697, exactly fifteen years to the day, the three children of the Witches of Bideford also met their end.

On the scaffold moments before the handle was pulled the overseeing priest, a reverend John Joyce, asked them to repent and did they have any last words. In unison the women shouted to the Bideford judge and to the watching and jeering crowd that they would all be cursed and that the women will return and wreak havoc on those around. With that the floor gave way and all that could be heard was the twang of a rope and the creaking of the scaffold.

For a whole day the corpses hung there, slowly swinging and twisting in the breeze till, just as dusk was falling and everyone had retreated back to their homes, a hunched up figure completely covered by an old tattered black cloak drove up to the scaffold on a dirty broken down old cart pulled by an emaciated black horse. The cloaked figure eased itself down from the cart and climbed the scaffold with a noticeable limp, to where the corpses hung. A couple of crows, that had been feasting on the eyes of the pathetic corpses, squawked and flew off, indignant that their meal had been interrupted. A thin scrawny blood-stained hand but with a large ring with a bright black stone set at its centre emerged from beneath the cloak. Gripped in the hand was a small dagger, again with a large black stone at the top of its hilt. The figure slashed at the ropes that formed the nooses which had been the demise of the three women and they all fell with a thud onto the ground below the scaffold. A cloud of flies suddenly erupted from the bloated bodies and buzzed around waiting to reclaim their food source. The black figure slowly and with great effort pulled each corpse along the dew-covered grass and onto the cart. When the last of his pathetic cargo had been boarded he climbed up onto the driver's bench and with a flick of the reins the tired looking horse pulled the cart out of the green and into the darkness of the night.

Nothing was heard or seen of the figure or the dead women for some time during which the whole episode was forgotten by the town's people. Occasionally, someone in the Bideford judge's household would make a snide remark as, despite his promises on the night of the murder, no one had received any monetary reward for their silence and perjury. In fact the judge had become even more obnoxious and tyrannical and spent much of his time searching through the records erasing any mention of the women, the trial and the hanging and especially any part that he had in it.

It was not until a year later, on the night of the 24th August 1698 that the weather began to change and the sky began to turn a deep shade of red. The wind started to increase making all the lanterns in the streets in both Bideford and Exeter swing on their hooks, squeaking and banging against the posts. Rain started to fall but not ordinary rain, this rain was red.

The people of the towns started to mutter and worry. They had never seen such weather in all their lives. Little children could sense the concern of the adults and many were heard crying with their mothers ushering them off the streets and into the protection of the houses. The storm increased throughout the night and into the next day, the 25th of August. Even at noon the sky was still so overcast with the blood-red clouds that made it impossible to see without a lantern. No-one ventured out.

At three in the afternoon, there was an incredible bolt of lightning which lit up the sky followed by the rumble and crash of thunder that seemed to go on for at least a minute. As it faded away it was replaced by a total silence then, without warning, the scream of a woman, closely followed by further screams and the crying of children. People started running out into the streets shouting murder and pleading for help. Little children and some even bigger ones were seen wandering the streets crying and shouting for their mummies. Grown men with obvious tears rolling down their faces wandered aimlessly up and down the roads all asking the same question. "What's been happening, my wife or son or daughter or brother or sister is dead. What can we do?" Someone suggested that they go to the judge's house and ask his advice, so a gathering of very distraught men, women and a few children all marched to the judge's mansion.

On arriving at the gates they were all surprised that everything was quiet. No lights shone out of the windows and despite the strong wind which was now calming down as the first chinks of sunlight penetrated through the dark red clouds, nothing moved in the garden, not even a branch of a tree. The crowd pushed open the large, ornate cast-iron gate surmounted by the crest and coat of arms of the judge's family. It gave an ominous creak and squeak. They jostled up to the front door and one man in the front of the throng banged on the large oak door with a large ball-ended cane he was carrying. The noise of the bang could be heard echoing through the corridors of the old manor house in which the judge lived. It was rumoured that he had won it in a card game from some old lord or something but the game had been fixed. Following its loss the old lord had thrown himself off Bideford long bridge into the river Torridge and drowned, his body never to be found.

The house remained silent. No noise of a servant rushing to open the door or any movement could be heard so the man with the cane struck the door again but this time with much more force. The anticipating crowd fell silent and listened for a sign that they would be allowed entry.

Silence! An owl suddenly screeched and flapped out of the branches of a nearby oak tree. The noise made everyone jump but it broke the silence and everyone started to murmur and ask their neighbour what was going on. The man with the cane pushed onto the door. It creaked and slowly opened. The man then pushed his head round the edge of the door and shouted "Hello, anyone----" He never got to say "at home" for there, lying on the stone flags of the entrance hall, were three figures all stretched out at weird angles. Two of the bodies were female, the servant girls of the house hold and one was male, the butler. All three had bulging eyes, protruding swollen tongues and a deep red wheal mark around their necks as if they had been strangled, or hanged.

The man with the cane told all the women to stay back and not to come in but one young girl could not contain her curiosity and pushed her way passed. She just made it through the door when she screamed with such intensity that the other people outside covered their ears with the discomfort. The girl swivelled and in one movement ran from the scene still screaming, her friends chasing after her asking what was wrong. The man then ordered all the women to go back to their respective houses while he and a few of the other men present pushed the big oak door fully open and went inside to survey the carnage that had obviously taken place. The men travelled down the corridors opening each door as they came to them and looking inside.

Almost, without exception, in every room they found the mutilated body of one or more of the household servants, all with the now characteristic deep red wheal mark around their necks. Finally the man with the cane came to the door of the judge's study. He had been there several times before and new it well as it was the room were the judge interrogated men, women and children who were accused of any misdemeanour. It had only been through bribery that he had persuaded the judge not to send him to prison for poaching. Fearing the judge's wrath at being disturbed he gently knocked on the door with his cane but since receiving no response he knocked harder. Still no reply! Gently turning the door knob he gingerly eased-open the door and peered inside. All looked perfectly normal and so he and another man, a candle-maker by trade, straightened up and made their way into the room. They had only advanced two paces when the candle-maker turned his head and gasped loudly. He found he could not speak and all he could do was to grab the coat of his companion and give it a sharp tug. The man with the cane turned to see what he wanted and at the same time saw the spectre before him. Lying on his back behind the door was the judge. He did not have the deep red wheal around his neck or at least not one that could be seen because his whole body was covered in blood and from the angles of his arms and legs they were obviously broken. His whole body had been beaten with such ferocity that it was impossible to tell were his clothes finished and his flesh began. A huge pool of blood had oozed from his body and formed a thick sticky mess on the floor and carpets around him. The two men jumped backwards to avoid standing in it. Lying across his chest was his heavy ball-ended cane. This had obviously been the weapon which had been used to beat him to death as it was splintered and caked in blood and by coincidence the same one that he himself had used to beat to death poor Stephen Floyd.

It was two days later that the news came to the still shocked Bideford townspeople that a similar murderous outpouring had occurred in Exeter where the bodies of the towns senior judge, the local executioner and many of the people that had witnessed and jeered at the hanging of the three witches a year earlier had all been found dead with deep rope burn marks around their necks.

Tales and rumours abounded for years after this happening to the point that every August 25th people in Bideford and Exeter used to shut themselves away or even move out of the area for a few days," To visit relatives you understand." they would say but everyone knew the real reason,

Since then little has been heard about the events on that night but every ten years on the night of August 24th the sky turns a deep blood -red and the wind seems to increase but just around Bideford centring on the site where the Judges house stood. Such were the tales about the happenings in the house that no one was prepared to live there and so it slowly crumbled away and with it its notorious history.

Hugo sat enthralled by the tale and urged Bird to tell him more but there was a noise outside of slamming car doors and the cheery voices saying "Bye, bye, thank you for coming." and "please call again soon". Even the voice of Stephanie floated up to his ears with "Bye Marty, I love you." which made Hugo feel decidedly sick. He turned back to Bird to entreat him to tell him more about the sisters and the witches and his own part in the story and how he ended trapped inside the zigzag stone but it had disappeared. All that was left were the two halves of the zigzag patterned rock from which Bird had emerged. Hugo picked up the pieces fitted the two halves together like a jigsaw piece and wrapped some sticky tape around them to hold them together and put the whole rock in pride of place in his toy cupboard. It was at this point that he heard his sister and parents saying goodnight to each other as they all prepared to come to bed. Hugo had been so intent on listening to the story that Bird had been relating that he had not yet undressed ready for bed. Since he used having an early night as an excuse to leave the unwelcome company of the Edmunds's he thought it best that he appear asleep when his mother or father popped their heads round his door to check he was all OK before they went to bed themselves so he quickly undressed put on his pyjamas and jumped into bed. His mother had put clean sheets on his bed that day and they felt cool and slippery to his skin as he snuggled down beneath the duvet. He suddenly remembered that he had not cleaned his teeth which would have greatly annoyed his father but he promised himself that he would clean them for twice as long in the morning to make up for it. The night was calm and despite Hugo being excited at all that had happened that day he rapidly fell fast asleep. It was the 11th of August.

CHAPTER 5

Emma Jones

Hugo woke up early the next day. He wasn't sure if all the adventure of yesterday had been real or just a dream. He threw back his duvet and jumped out of bed. Pulling back his curtains, which he assumed one of his parents must have closed after he had gone to sleep as he had certainly not closed them, he saw that the morning was bright with only a few fluffy clouds in the sky. He rushed over to his toy cupboard and sure enough there was the zigzag stone with its sheath of sticky tape still lying in the place he had left it the night before. "Well at least that part of yesterday was true." he thought to himself. Just at that moment Jake nosed his way round the door thinking that since someone was up and about there might be some food in the offing. He squirmed his way around Hugo's legs almost knocking him over. He jumped up an licked and slobbered over Hugo's face until Hugo could stand it no longer and grabbing his dressing gown from behind his door he made his way downstairs, almost tripping over his dressing gown belt as he went. Jake bounded ahead and into the kitchen anticipating the treats that were to come as Hugo was always a soft touch as far as Jake was concerned and he knew that if he pawed Hugo's arm long enough that he would get an extra doggy chew. This was frowned upon by Mrs Bennett who was fastidious about dietary control for Jake as well as the family. "We're not going to become another statistic in the obesity reports." She frequently used to say. This was triggered when she noticed Stephanie becoming a little podgy while she was "in love" with Justin in Reading but she didn't want to make too big a thing of it in case Stephanie herself became obsessed and resorted to anorexia. So much of it was heard about in the press these days.

Hugo finally succumbed to Jakes pawing and persistent attention and threw him the extra doggy chew which Jake deftly caught in mid-air then sloped off to his basket to enjoy. Hugo meanwhile, busied himself by pouring out a bowl of Cheerios. He preferred Sugar Puffs but his dad had to practice what he preached and it was only on very rare occasions, usually when his grandparents stayed and they did the shopping, that he was ever allowed these forbidden sugar coated delicacies. So today he'd have to make do with Cheerios. He opened the fridge door and took out a carton of milk, "skimmed" of course because "it's healthier?" casually noticing that there were large holes in the packet containing the cheese. Also several of the tops of the yogurt pots had been pierced and the pots seemed half full. These facts did not fully register with Hugo at that time as the bowl of Cheerios sitting on the kitchen table was being closely eyed up by Jake who had wolfed down his own doggy chew and was now eager to find out what else was on the menu.

At this point Mr Bennett came into the kitchen rubbing his eyes, scratching his head and yawning. "'orning" he said half way through his yawn, "you're up early today." and proceeded to fill the kettle to make himself and his wife a cup of tea.

"Yes." said Hugo, "since I went to bed early last night I woke up early this morning and it's such a nice day outside I thought that it would be a shame to waste it."

"Humph." snorted his dad. "It's a pity you're not so enthusiastic about getting up early when its school time." As Hugo knew that he was always the last to get out of bed in the mornings which often made him nearly late for school.

Hugo just sniffed and finished eating his Cheerios. His father finished filling the teapot and went across to the fridge to get the milk. He opened the door, reached in and grabbed the milk carton. He was just shutting the door when he stopped and opened it up again wide. "What in the worlds been happening in here!" he exclaimed.

"What d'you mean?" Hugo replied, his mouth still full with Cheerios.

"I think we must have mice or something. Look at the state of these yoghurts and what's been at this lump of cheese? Have you been messing about in here?" Hugo's father asked accusingly.

"No I haven't." retorted Hugo, spraying Cheerios over the table.

"Well something or someone has been at this fridge. You wait till I catch those responsible. All this food will have to be thrown away." "Typical of dad." thought Hugo," he hates the thought of wasting food."

"Well go and get dressed." Hugo's father said with annoyance "and don't forget to clean your teeth!"

Hugo had forgotten that he had not cleaned his teeth the night before so he picked up his now empty bowl and placed it in the dishwasher much to the annoyance of Jake who was anticipating licking it out, a thing which Hugo would have let him do if his father had not been around. Jake slouched back to his basket, his tail, hanging loosely, between his legs.

When Hugo reached the top of the stairs he turned to go into the bathroom to clean his teeth but the door was locked and Stephanie's voice shouted from within, "I'm in here."

"Drat it." thought Hugo, for he knew that once Stephanie entered the bathroom in the mornings she'd be in there for what seemed an eternity. "I don't know what she does in there all this time," thought Hugo. "It's not as if she looks any better when she comes out than when she went in? She still looks ugly." This is generally referred to brotherly love and the feelings were equally reciprocated, at least on the outside.

Hugo returned to his bedroom and once more took out the stone from his toy cupboard. "Pretty isn't it." a familiar voice said from behind his door. Hugo swung around so rapidly that it made his head swim. "Bird!" he exclaimed almost dropping the stone. "I thought I'd been dreaming." He said ecstatically.

"Don't speak so loudly." whispered Bird. "I'm only supposed to speak to children."

"Well" responded Bird "As you can see I am not your normal average bird and adults always get worried and sometimes frightened if they come across something or someone that, let us say, is not what you'd normally see on a daily basis. In the past I've had some very close scrapes with grown-ups so that now I stay as clear as possible of them as I can. Oh by the way, have you got anything to eat? I'm starving. All I've had is a bit of cheese and some yoghurt."

"It was you! It was you!" exclaimed Hugo "It was you who messed up all the food in the fridge last night. My dad accused me but I denied it and said it must be rats or a very big mouse."

"I'm sorry." Said Bird but I've been trapped in that egg for ages and ages and I felt a bit peckish last night."

"Stay here." ordered Hugo and rewrapping his dressing gown around himself he started back down into the kitchen. He could still hear Stephanie splashing around in the bathroom trying, "in vain." Hugo thought, as he rushed past the bathroom door but he couldn't resist the temptation to bang loudly on the door and shout "Hurry up ugly." as he went passed.

"Go away you smelly dog." Shouted back his sister and he heard something heavy hit the door.

Ignoring the insult he carried on and ran down the stairs into the kitchen. He saw that his father was no longer there as he had made the tea and taken a cup up to his wife to drink in bed. Hugo seized his chance. He swung open the fridge door and grabbed all the pots of yoghurt he could find even those that still had their lids intact. He also seized the block of cheese with the holes in the packet and stacked everything onto the table. He then added to his haul the remains of the carton of milk his father had used for making the tea, the remains of a loaf of bread from the bread bin, "It was going stale anyway." Hugo reassured himself and finally for good measure he picked up the box of Cheerios, pulled out the inner bag containing the goodies and carefully replaced the empty box back into the kitchen cupboard where the cereals were usually kept. Looking round he spied an old Morrison's carrier bag in a corner. Tearing at it he went over to the kitchen table and piled everything in. He forgot to put the top on the milk carton and milk splashed all over yoghurts and cheese. "Never mind "thought Hugo "it's all dairy." And with that he picked up the bag and rushed back up the stairs and into his bedroom.

Stephanie heard him rushing up the stairs and recognising his heavy pounding footsteps shouted out from within the bathroom, "Nearly finished." But Hugo was too preoccupied to care.

Once ensconced in his bedroom Hugo quietly closed the door and looked around for Bird but he was nowhere to be seen. Suddenly the wall at the foot of Hugo's bed began to shimmer and Bird materialised as if by magic. Well it was magic really as Bird tied to explain to the gobsmacked Hugo.

"Well I told you I was not an ordinary bird. Now where's the food. I'm so hungry I could eat a witch."

"A witch?" Hugo queried. "Well not a whole one perhaps but I could make a good start."

With that Bird stuck his head into the carrier bag and didn't take it out until all that remained were a load of empty yoghurt pots, a scrunched up cheese wrapper, an almost empty carton of milk and a few odd Cheerios. "I prefer Sugar Puffs really." belched Bird.

"Oh so do I." agreed Hugo looking surprised but we only get them when my grand- parents come down and smuggle them in.

He looked up as if to ask Bird a question when without looking at any clock Bird announced, "My my, is that the time? Must dash. See you later, some friends of mine are in a spot of bother and I need to sort things out." With that, he suddenly blended back into the wall and was gone.

At that very moment a shout was heard from the bathroom "Finished" and the door to the bathroom opened and in a cloud of steam Stephanie emerged like Venus. Well not quite like Venus, more like a white bathrobe topped with a pink towel wrapped round her head and big fluffy slippers shaped like cats. Hugo was right, what did she do in the bathroom all that time and still look a mess when she got out?

Hugo waited for the steam and the smell of Stephanie's deodorant, or that's what she called it but Hugo thought it should be called "oderant" because it certainly did not take smells away, quite the opposite, to dissipate and then went in to wash his face, or at least make it wet so that his mother will think it's been washed, and clean his teeth. He remembered now that he had not brushed them last night and so gave them an extra really hard scrub. However, when he spat out the toothpaste he noticed that there was quite a considerable amount of blood mixed with the spit. He had seen adverts on the TV about people seeing blood in their spit and losing all their teeth. He did not relish the idea of this and so to be on the safe side he would ask his dad if there was anything wrong when he got back home from work.

The day seemed to drag and Hugo could not settle as he waited for the return of Bird and his father. He did not know which he wanted to see first. As it happened it was his father. He came home a little earlier than normal and after he settled down with a cup of coffee in his favourite chair to read his newspaper. Hugo approached him and asked him if bleeding teeth were signs of a problem. His father, surprised at his son's sudden interest in his job, started to give a mini lecture on gum disease and all its repercussions, however he rapidly realised that Hugo was not the slightest bit interested and so asked him why he was asking the question. Hugo explained sheepishly about spitting out some blood when he cleaned his teeth that morning so his father got up, went over to his brief case and withdrew a small dentist's mouth mirror with a flourish. "Sit in the chair near the window and let's have a gander." He said so Hugo moved over to the chair nearest the window and threw is head back. His father stood behind him and peered down into his mouth. He wiggled the mirror around a few time and then announced, "I can see that you'll be having a visit from the Toothfairy soon. Your upper left D is about to fall out.".

"What's a D" questioned Hugo. "Oh, it's the baby tooth near the back. You remember last year your front tooth fell out and you were upset because you swallowed it, well the ones at the back are doing the same and your new teeth will grow into their place. I can also see that I might have to do some orthodontics on you in the future."

"I don't want those horrible braces that you fitted to Steph last year, lots of kids have got them at school and everyone makes fun of them, calling them Jaws or something."

"Don't worry," his dad replied "they've brought out some new invisible ones now that you can hardly see. I am going on a course in a month's time to learn how to use them and when I come back you can be my first victim." He made an evil face as he said the word victim but then smiled and rubbed Hugo on the head ruffling his hair.

His father put the mirror in a small plastic bag and placed it back in his briefcase and then went back to his chair and picked up the local newspaper again. As he shook the paper flattening it to read Hugo happened to glimpse the headlines;

Time Team to visit Bideford

Old "Judges" house to be excavated.

As soon as Hugo saw the word Judge he remembered the story that Bird had told him the night before. Kneeling at his father's feet he tried to read what was written below the headlines while his dad was concentrating on the inside pages. "What on earth are you doing?" his father enquired as soon as he realised that he was sharing his newspaper. "Oh," responded Hugo, "Someone was telling me a story about the old Judge's house recently and I was interested to learn what it was all about."

"Well from what I read," his father said, putting down his newspaper, "it seems that some local big wig has been tracing his ancestry and found that he was a distant relative of a judge that lived in a house that stood in that big plot of land just outside Bideford on the way to Torrington. It also seems that somehow he has managed to inherit the plot and wants to rebuild a house on the site. However, when he put in for planning permission it seems that the site has some historical interest. The house that originally stood there was part of an old abbey. The local archaeological group showed an interest and someone contacted the Time Team people off the tele, a programme that excavates archaeological sites over three days and they want to come down and excavate the site before it is lost under a load of new buildings. Oh, and there were a load of murders there!" whispered his dad and shook his paper as if to frighten Hugo but he did not have to pretend to be frightened for after what Bird had told him he genuinely was scared.

An hour later Hugo's dad had finished with the paper and so Hugo took it, spread it on the floor and began to read. Sure enough what his father had told him was true and that the Time Team people were coming down and were going to start filming the excavation on the 18th of that month which was just seven days before the exact anniversary of when the witches were hanged. Hugo couldn't wait to tell the news to Bird. Where was he? He had not seen him all that day.

The weather had turned dull and overcast in the afternoon and it was only with persistent nagging and threatening that Hugo had been persuade to take Jake out for his afternoon walk. However, half way round the route it started to rain and so Hugo started to run so that he didn't get wet. Jake loved this as he always enjoyed running rather than be kept restrained on a leash. By the time Hugo and Jake returned back home they were both quite wet and Hugo was out of breath. As soon as they both got through the door Jake shook himself violently so that Hugo was splattered with water and became even wetter. "Go and change your clothes." Hugo's mother shouted from within the kitchen from where a beautiful aroma of fresh bread was emanating. Mr Bennett had bought his wife a bread making machine as a Christmas present the year before and now despite a slow start Mrs Bennett was quite the expert. Her bread and rolls straight out of the machine were far better that the doughy rubbish they bought from the supermarket and it always made the house smell nice. Hugo went up to change while Jake went into the kitchen where he could be heard lapping up the water from his bowl and then settling down to crunch on his doggy chew.

When Hugo opened his bedroom door he saw Bird sat on the end of his bed eating some biscuits that Hugo had hidden in his drawer for "emergency" "Hey! those are mine," said Hugo. "And very nice they are to." replied Bird spitting crumbs over Hugo.

"Where have you been?" enquired Hugo. "Oh, I've been to see my friends, the Gnomes." Bird responded "they've got quite a nice little community. In fact it's not far from here. It's called the Gnome Reserve."

"I've heard of it." Said Hugo, "but I thought that it was just a lot of models scattered around someone's garden".

"Ah, that's what it looks like to ordinary people but the gnomes are very clever as they make models of themselves which they leave around so that they can move around more freely. If anyone sees them all they have to do is stand perfectly still and no one can tell the difference. Well except the lady who owns the garden but she's on the gnome's side and so doesn't let on that she knows which the real ones are to the visitors. In return they help to keep her garden tidy which is why you see the gnomes with spades and wheelbarrows."

"The gnomes are very worried" Bird went on. "quite a few of their number have started to go missing and last week Barguff, one of the older Gnomes came back exhausted saying that he had just escaped from Kadavera, an evil witch that inhabits a secret cave somewhere along the coast here. He had run so hard that he had not paid attention from where he had come. All he knew that it was in the direction of this house. What's more while he was imprisoned in the cave he heard the calls and cries of other Gnomes, so the Gnomes at the reserve have asked me to help find and rescue their friends from the witch. One thing Barguff did find out is that Kadavera is trying to find a potion that will allow her to exist in daylight as at present sunlight is the only thing that will kill her and if she can ever develop a daylight potion then she will take over the world."

Hugo slumped down on his bed both enthralled and terrified at what he had heard from Bird, especially about the part where Kadavera may be living close to where he was.

"Well what have you been up to?" asked Bird. Hugo was slow to reply as he was still stunned by what Bird had said but then suddenly remembering his news, he couldn't wait to tell Bird. He wriggled into the corner of his bed to make himself comfortable and then related all that he had read in the newspaper. This time is was Birds turn to be shocked.

"Oh my dearie dearie me he said that is definitely not good news. That house is cursed and I really do not know what will happen if any attempt is made to disturb it." Then Hugo added his piece de resistance. "They're going to start work on the 18th of August."

Suddenly the purple streak down Bird's head and body started rapidly changing through all the colours of the rainbow. Had it not been the shocked expression on Birds face it would have looked quite beautiful but as it was it made Hugo feel very worried.

"I am sorry but I need to see some friends about this." said Bird and suddenly evaporated in shimmer of colour.

Hugo sat on his bed for some time until a drop of rain that had lodged itself in his hair dripped off and ran chillily down his back. This brought him back into consciousness and he now realised how wet and cold he had become. Picking up a towel from the end of his bed he rubbed his hair and face dry and then threw off his wet clothes and put on clean dry ones from his cupboard. Kicking his wet clothes and the towel under his bed he ambled downstairs and into the warm lounge where Jake lay sprawled in the centre of the carpet. His still wet tail wagged and flapped as Hugo came into the room but he had found the only spot in the room where the now breaking sunshine was and was refusing to budge. Stephanie was watching one of her girly programmes on the TV and so Hugo jumped into his father's favourite chair, picked up the copy of the North Devon Journal in which he had read about the visit of Time Team and proceeded to reread to the article. He mumbled to Stephanie "Did you know that Time Team was coming to Bideford?" "Uh! What's that?" she mumbled back totally disinterested, engrossed in her programme where one of the actors was her heart throb and not a bad word could be said against him even though, as far as Hugo was concerned, he couldn't act, couldn't sing and looked like a big drip.

"What was that you said about Time Team?" asked his mother loudly from inside the kitchen. Time Team was one of her favourite programmes and she was an armchair archaeologist, though she did admit that the thought of all that digging, especially when it was cold and wet, was definitely not her cup of tea." Hugo eased himself out of the chair and paper in hand, took it into the kitchen to show his mother. She stopped washing up, dried her hands, took the newspaper and spread it out on the kitchen top. "Can I have a roll please mum?" said Hugo. "Oh yes." Said his mum and so Hugo picked up one of the hot crispy bread rolls that stood on plate on the kitchen worktop. His stomach rumbled and his mouth salivated at the prospect of biting into this tasty manna but as he sank his teeth into the warm crust he howled out in pain.

"What on earth is wrong?" said his mother dropping the newspaper and rushing over to Hugo's side. When she looked she could see that covering the top of the bread roll where Hugo had bitten was a great streak of blood. She put her hand to her mouth thinking that she had mixed some glass in with the dough and it had cut Hugo's mouth. "Don't worry mum." Hugo said and opening his mouth still full of crumbs and half eaten bread, he touched one of his baby teeth, the upper left D he thought to himself, between his fingers and gave it a big wiggle. A drop of blood mixed with saliva and bread crumbs dripped out of his mouth and onto the floor. "Well that's a relief." Breathed his mother and wiping her hands down onto her pinafore she walked back to the paper and continued to read. While she had her head buried in the paper Hugo reached out and took another bread roll, in case Bird felt hungry again, and went up to his room to finish his own roll but this time he took care to bite on the other side and do it very carefully.

He started to play a game on his computer but didn't really feel in the mood so he kneeled on his bed looking out of the window and absent-mindedly wiggled his loose tooth. Suddenly, the tooth came out in his fingers. He stared at it for a moment and then rushed downstairs and shouted to his mother, "Mum, mum look what's happened." He held the small white object between his thumb and forefinger up into his mother's face and smiled with a big broad grin like a chimpanzee to prove that he had a new gap where the tooth had been. "Oh that's great" said his mother. "It's a pity, your dad was quite looking forward to taking that out." That sent a shiver down Hugo's back for even though his dad was a dentist he still did not relish the thought of having a tooth out, especially not after all the tales the children had told him at school in full blood curdling detail. "Don't forget to put it under your pillow tonight. You never know, the Toothfairy might come." his mother added. "Now go up to your room and wash your hands, your daddy will be home soon and we've got your favourite for dinner tonight and treacle pudding with custard for afters." Hugo's favourite was in fact his mum's home-made shepherd's pie with roast potatoes and gravy. His mum always spoilt it though by always serving it with cabbage which he hated but was forced to eat by his dad who said that greens were good for you. So he had learned to smother the cabbage with gravy so that it would mask the taste and eat it, or as much as he thought he could get away with, quickly right at the beginning of the meal so that the rest of the shepherd's pie would take away the disgusting taste.

Hugo turned and ran up to his room rolling the small tooth between his fingers. As he opened the door he dropped the small object and it took him several minutes on his hands and knees scrabbling under his bed before he found it again. He was amazed how much rubbish there was under his bed. He even found the missing part of his F16 fighter plane model that had meant that the model was always tilted as the missing part was the left undercarriage. "Great." thought Hugo and picked it up and repositioned it back in its rightful place on the model making it stand straight for the first time in months. He then lifted the pillow on his bed and carefully positioned his tiny tooth underneath but close to the edge so that his mum or his dad could easily exchange it for some money during the night while he was asleep. He still pretended to believe in the Toothfairy especially when it meant that he would get an extra pound pocket money that week. "You never know," he thought to himself, "I may even get a two pound coin this time." Most of the boys at school bragged that this is what they got but Hugo knew for a fact that this was a lie though he could not prove it.

At dinner, amongst the conversation, Mrs Bennett announced to Hugo that Emma Jones would be coming round and staying the next day and that Hugo must be nice to her as her father had been taken seriously ill and her mother had to travel to Bristol, about 100 miles away to be with him and there was no one else to look after her. Emma Jones was a girl from Hugo's class. He did not really know her as the boys never mixed with the girls. It just wasn't done. After all they're "girls", and she had only recently joined the class having moved down from London a few months before. She was about the same height as Hugo with straight brown hair but that was all Hugo could remember about her. She was very quiet and sat behind Hugo in the classroom and so he never had the opportunity to look at her much. Hugo was definitely not pleased with this news. Admitted, he was getting a bit bored, having to entertain himself during the summer holidays, which seemed to be going on and on, as his best friend and normal playmate, Paul Friendship, had gone to Spain on holiday with his parents but to have to share his day with a girl was a real nightmare. Hugo was a little jealous of Paul's holiday as it meant that Paul would be flying in a real aeroplane, something Hugo had yet to do.

"Oh do I really have to?" moaned Hugo at which point Stephanie piped up "Hugo's getting a girlfriend. Hugo's getting a girlfriend!"

"That's enough of that." Mr Bennett said sternly and Stephanie suddenly fell silent.

The rest of the evening Hugo sulked around the lounge making sure that everyone knew that he was very unhappy at the thought of having to entertain a girl. Even Jake was pushed away when he came over to be stroked. At eight o'clock Hugo mumbled that he was going to bed and without wishing anyone goodnight stomped his way up the stairs to his room where he slammed the door shut. His parents looked at each other, sighed and went back to reading and watching the television.

Hugo was in such a bad mood that he quite forgot about Bird or his tooth under the pillow. He tossed off his clothes, throwing them untidily on the floor, put on his pyjamas and threw himself into bed dreading having to spend the next day with a girl. What would Paul and his other friends say when they heard? It was with much tossing and shuffling in his bed that he finally drifted off to sleep.

He awoke next morning to the sound of a car drawing up outside their house and the doors banging shut. A moment later the doorbell sounded and he could hear the noise of the front door being unlocked. "Oh hello

Miriam and you must be Emma?" he heard his mother's welcoming voice ring out. "Would you like a cup of tea or something?" she asked. "Oh no," Mrs Jones replied as Hugo assumed it to be. "I must rush off. I have a long journey and I want to try to beat the early-morning rush." Turning to her daughter she said. "Now don't forget what I told you. Do whatever Mrs Bennett tells you to do and don't get into trouble." "Yes mum." The young girl mumbled and walked slowly under Mrs Bennett's arm as she held the door open for her. "I really do appreciate you helping me out and looking after Emma for me Julia. I shall try and be back as soon as possible. If there are any problems then please give me a call on my mobile. I think you have the number?" "That's quite alright." his mum replied. "I'm sure that Emma here will be no trouble and yes I do have your mobile number."

With that, Mrs Jones bent down, kissed her daughter on the cheek, turned and climbed into her car, a bright red Ferrari. "What a smashing car." Hugo thought to himself as he eased himself out of bed and looked out of the bedroom window. "I wish my dad had one like that." At the same time his opinion of Emma started to climb. Still reluctant to meet his companion for that day he took his time dressing. He even let the timer on his electric toothbrush actually get to the end when he cleaned his teeth. Definitely a first. However, his stomach was telling him that it needed filling so reluctantly he went down stairs.

"Good morning Hugo. This is Emma. She's come to stay with us for today. I told you yesterday." "Hello" mumbled Hugo without making eye contact. "Hello" replied Emma, equally subdued. "Well that's fine." said Hugo's Mother. "What would you both like for breakfast?" "Cheerios" murmured Hugo. "And you Emma?" "Yes please" she replied. With that Mrs Bennett went over to the cupboard and took out the box of Cheerios but as she opened the packet she gasped. "Well that's odd, there's only an empty box here. I am sure it was almost full yesterday. Do you know anything about it?" she asked accusingly of Hugo. "Nothing to do with me." He lied, "but I'll have cornflakes instead if there aren't any Cheerios." he went on trying to avoid further questioning and change the subject. "Well I'm very sorry," Hugo's mother said apologetically turning to Emma "will cornflakes be OK for you? Or we do have Weetabix." "Cornflakes will be fine thank you." she sheepishly replied. The meal was spent in silence except for Mrs Bennett asking Emma about the things she liked and what were her interests but her responses were short and not particularly informative.

"Why don't you take Emma to your room and show her that new computer game you've been going on about. You kept moaning that it was better if two people played it." Without reply Hugo started up to his room with Emma, equally reluctantly, following him. "Don't forget to tidy it either and make your bed." a voice cried out from the kitchen. It was met with stony silence. The two children slouched up the stairs, Emma staying several feet behind Hugo. He opened his bedroom door and went in. Emma stayed at the doorway. "What a mess!" she exclaimed. "So what." Responded Hugo and started kicking all the clothes he had taken off the night before and which still lay on the floor, under the bed. As he did so he dislodged the stone with the zigzag pattern and it rolled into the centre of the room. Emma jumped on it to stop it rolling and picked it up, carefully rolling it around and examining it. "That's mine!" shouted Hugo "Give it me. It's private" and made a lunge for it wrenching it out of Emma's hand. "What's so special about a silly old stone?" she said sarcastically. "I said it's private." Retorted Hugo, pulling the stone close to his chest and sitting down heavily onto his bed. The sudden bounce of his body onto the bed dislodged his pillow and it fell to the floor. The eagle-eyed Emma then said "and what's that?" pointing to where the pillow had just lain. Hugo turned round and looked at where Emma was pointing and noticed the small object lying on the sheet. He had quite forgotten his tooth but now that he saw it he remembered but felt quite disappointed that it was still there and not replaced by a shiny new one pound, or even better two pound, coin. "It's my tooth" he said. "It fell out yesterday and I put it under my pillow to see if my mum or dad would swop it for some money." "No, not the silly old tooth, I could see what that is" Emma responded "I meant that that little tiny piece of paper over there."

Hugo looked again to where his tooth was and sure enough about three inches away lay a small piece of pink paper. It looked like it had been torn from the corner of a book or something and did not really register with Hugo, but Emma reached out and picked it up from the sheet. "Well, what is it?" Hugo insisted. "I don't know but there is some writing on it but it is very small." the young girl replied. "Let me see." said Hugo almost tearing the paper from her hand but even he found the writing too small to read. "I know" proclaimed Hugo and started to rummage through the drawer in his cupboard, finally raising his hand with a flourish. "Got it!" In his hand he held a large magnifying glass which he proceeded to use to try and read the writing. "Bet it says made in China or something." he murmured to himself. "Let me see. Let me see." insisted Emma and craned her head over Hugo's to see what was written. It took a little time, moving the magnifying glass backwards and forwards, till they could see what was scrawled on the paper in very fine hand writing.

Please Help me. T F

"What does that mean Hugo" asked Emma "and who or what is T F?" "I've absolutely no idea." Hugo replied but now in his normal voice and not the grunts and single syllable words he had been using up to this point. The discovery of a mutual query had made him forget that he was talking to a "girl."

They passed the small piece of paper between themselves together with the magnifying glass, reading and rereading the message but not understanding what it meant. "Well I've never seen it before." Hugo assured Emma but it sounds like T F is in trouble. They posed question after question to each other for quite some time till they ran out of questions to ask and so Emma asked Hugo if she could look at the new game he had on his computer. "It's a car racing game." Hugo proudly announced and booted up his computer that stood in the corner of his room on a desk supporting a large flat-screen monitor. When it suddenly appeared on the screen it showed a bright red Ferrari racing against a dark green Aston Martin. "That's like your mum's." Hugo said pointing to the screen with a noticeable hint of envy in his voice. "You must be pretty rich to have one of those." "Oh I wish," said Emma. "that was not my mum's car. She works for a big car showroom in Exeter and they had a customer who lives in Bristol who had left his car where she works to be serviced but he needed it back in a hurry. When the boss heard that my mum was having to drive to Bristol today he had asked her if she could drive the Ferrari and drop it off at the customer's office and she would then come home by train. Your dad has arranged to pick her up at the station."

This made Hugo feel much better. He knew he could not match someone whose family was wealthy enough to own a Ferrari. Deep down this made Emma more equal to Hugo who even he had to admit to himself lacked the confidence and bravado of some of the other boys in his class. While he was still engrossed rereading the tiny note she noticed the zigzag stone again. Hugo had put it down on the bed while he searched for the magnifying glass. Picking it up, she rolled it round in her hands, fiddling with the sticky tape as she did so. The tape suddenly became detached from one half of the stone and it separated and fell to the floor with a thud. Hugo was immediately on the defensive again and tore the one half out of Emma's hands shouting at her to leave it alone it was his and private. She blushed and said sorry and bent down to pick up the fallen half. As she gathered it up from the floor she looked at it and then stopped. "What's written inside?" she asked. "What d'you mean?" Hugo replied as he went to snatch this half from her. "Well there's some strange writing on the inside. Hugo stopped short. Although he had thoroughly examined the outside of the stone when he acquired it he had never bothered to look on the inside and now more carefully and politely he took the second half and looked inside. Sure enough, etched into the inner wall of the stone was a mass of squiggles and what almost looked like Egyptian Hieroglyphics. Now that Hugo looked there were some on the inside of his half as well. They looked at each other dumbfounded, each asking each other what it all meant, but without actually speaking. They both sat on the bed turning and twisting each half in their hands trying to fathom what the inscription said or meant. "There's one bit here" Emma finally spoke up "that looks a bit like English and it is repeated several times between the two halves."

"Let's see?" chimed in Hugo and they both peered into the shell. Emma pointed at the part where she had been looking and they both slowly spelt out PHILATITROCUSFUMARITOR. "What in the world does that mean?" Emma queried and both of them slowly said it again trying to see if it made any sense. They had just finished repeating it for the third time when the wall of Hugo's bedroom shimmered and Bird emerged from out of nowhere.

Emma dropped the half of the stone that she had been holding, screamed and jumped backwards onto the bed pulling the duvet as tightly around her as possible. "Is everything alright?" a voice sounded from down the bottom of the stairs. "Everything's OK." Hugo quickly responded "Emma's lost a race." "At least they seem to getting on alright" Hugo's mother thought to herself. "That's a relief." and returned to her ironing.

"I'm very sorry to have surprised you." Bird said apologetically to Emma, "hasn't Hugo told you about me?" "No he certainly hasn't." she said loudly, now getting some of her courage back. "Let me introduce myself to you. I am called Ostricoelephantidae Philatitrocusfumaritor Minor or an Ostricoelephantasaurus for short" he said with a sort of high pitched screech which did not sound a bit like with the way they had said it. "most people call me Bird as they never make the sound of my name properly but you both did pretty well. I think that I get my name from looking a bit like an ostrich but with the ears of an elephant but I think mine are much nicer. Don't you think? Since you said my name three times I decided to come to see if there was a problem. Without realising it Emma had moved up to Hugo and was trying to hold onto him. Hugo was beginning to accept the company of his new female friend but actual physical contact was a way beyond acceptability and quickly moved away and stood up. "Hi Bird." he said, regaining his composure. "we didn't actually call you but we noticed," "I noticed." interrupted Emma. "OK, when Emma noticed the writing on the inside of your egg but the only bit we could read was Phila-whatever it is." "Ah yes "said Bird thoughtfully." What does it all mean?" continued Hugo.

"Well "said Bird, "it's my life story. As I told you yesterday I had been in that stone for a long time and while I was inside I scratched my life story on the inside just in case I never survived and also to pass the time. Unfortunately, although I could learn to speak your language by listening through the rock I could not see through enough to see how you wrote it down so I used the writing of my own country plus a mix of what I picked up before I became trapped in the stone. It was a bit cramped so it was difficult to write properly." Well what does it all say"

Emma enquired as her courage slowly returned. "It was like this;" began Bird settling down on his haunches, fluffing his wings and stretching his neck.

"I was born or hatched as a normal Ostrich in the year 1691 and spent my formative years running around the plains of Africa like any normal ostrich. One day I was happily sleeping in the warm sunshine when a net was thrown over me and my older brother and we were bundled into a wooden crate. The crate was taken and loaded onto a big ship and we sailed for many days over what turned out to be a very rough sea. When the boat reached port I found myself in England. We were sold to a troupe of fairground people who used to exhibit us as strange and exotic animals from darkest Africa in their traveling show. It wasn't a bad life, we were fed regularly and except in the middle of winter, were kept warm.

It was in 1697, in August, in a place called Exeter, which I believe is not far from here, that we were quietly resting after being shown for a couple of days after a special event, a hanging I think, that a dark figure, covered in a thick black cloak and driving an rickety old cart, came by and stole us from our owners. The figure threw us in the back of the cart and drove away for what seemed all night. When we had recovered from being thrown in the cart I looked around and was shocked to see that alongside me were the corpses of three women who had obviously been hanged as they still had the remains of the nooses around their necks. Their faces were grossly distorted as a result of the crows pecking at them. The only thing that stood out was that each had an identical ring on their right hand with a large round stone in each except that one stone was red, one blue and one green.

As dawn was breaking the cart stopped and the black figure got off it and hoisted us and the corpses into a dirty old cave. As the figure held the sack I was in I noticed that he also had a ring like the corpses except his was jet black.

Days went by and we were left in the sack without food or water. I could hear lots of weird incantations with load bangs and horrible smells when suddenly there was a bright flash of lightening followed by a deafening crash of thunder and then absolute silence. Minutes went by when I heard a funny sort of shuffling and three cloaked figures came and threw me into a cage. I could not easily see their faces in the dim light but I did notice that each figure wore an identical ring with only the colour of the stone being different. One was red, one blue and one green. The dark figure with the black ring was nowhere to be seen.

During the weeks, months and years that passed they fed us many strange potions and used us and a variety of other animals especially gnomes and fairies as they are like humans but smaller, to try out their experiments to allow them to go out in daylight. From what I heard they had been resurrected with a special potion but it did not allow them to go out into daylight. They were so desperate that they tried mixing potions made from the bodies of one animal to another. What you see is the result. One of their potions went wrong and made me appear as if I was dead and so they fashioned a rock, reduced me in size and sealed me inside. They apparently did this to all the animals and creatures they killed so that they could dispose of us on the nearby beach without raising any suspicion. They would wait until it was dark then venture out from the cave where they were hiding and throw us as far as they could into the sea. Sometime after they had thrown me away there was a big storm and it washed my rock up onto and over the beach and into a rabbit hole, where I remained until you found me. During my imprisonment in the rock the effect of the witch's potion wore off and I woke up but I also found that the mixture of potions I had received while in captivity had left me with some special powers so I found that I can now become invisible, fly and lots of other funny stuff. My brother was similarly transformed but his rock ended up as ballast on a ship and this is why he ended up in Tasmania, however, one of the potions he was given made him grow to an enormous size which stopped him flying and he now pretends to be one of the hills where he lives, only emerging when no one is around."

During the tale both Emma and Hugo leant forward so as not to miss one word but as Bird finished talking they fell back exhausted with excitement. "Who and what are these three witches?" asked Emma. "Haven't you told her?" Bird retorted looking at Hugo who then blushed and looked sheepish. So Bird quickly repeated the story of the three women who were hanged and the disappearance of their bodies. Emma was quite shocked and shuffled and jiggled around not knowing how to react until Bird turned to her and said "And who are you young lady?" "Oh, I'm Emma, Emma Jones. My dad has been taken ill and Hugo's mum is looking after me while my mum visits him in Bristol." "Sorry to hear about your father." said Bird who then turned to Hugo and asked him what he'd been doing. Hugo was about to speak when Emma interrupted and almost shouted, "We found this." and passed over the small pink piece of paper to Bird who very dexterously took it in the tips of his wings. "It's got some writing on it asking for help," she continued. Bird started studying the paper and with his expression becoming more serious he asked where it had been found. "It was under my pillow next to my tooth." Hugo jumped up and grimaced at Bird at the same time to show him where the tooth had come from. "but the Toothfairy never came though." He added very dejectedly. There's a very good reason for that," Bird responded with a very serious tone in his voice. "This note is from the Toothfairy, see T F, and I have a very bad feeling that something very untoward has happened to her. Before I came here I was visiting the gnomes and they told me that one of their number, a gnome called Barguff, had been captured by a witch called Kadavera who was living in a cave not far away. He had managed to escape before she had had any chance to try out her potions on him but while he was shut away in a box he had heard the noises and cries of lots of other creatures. He specifically said that he thought he heard the name of the Toothfairy mentioned and if he is right then that may be the reason your tooth wasn't exchanged."

"You mean that there really is a Toothfairy, I thought that it was a fairy story to please small children?" interrupted Emma. Bird looked down at her with a very stern expression but said nothing gazing out of the window deep in thought. At that moment footsteps could be heard coming up the stairs and a knock sounded on Hugo's door. Bird suddenly vanished and quickly Emma and Hugo spun round to look as if they had been playing on the computer which conveniently was still running the game programme of car racing. "I've brought you up a snack. Thought you might be getting hungry." announced Mrs Bennett as she poked her head around the door and came into the room.

She had a tray with a plate of sandwiches, two small chocolate marshmallows and two glasses of orange squash which she put down on the table next to Hugo's bed. "Who's winning?" she asked and both Emma and Hugo answered at the same time "I am!" "Well, it's sort of a draw." said Hugo to avoid any further questioning. "Well, that's fine, I'm glad to see that you're enjoying yourselves." Hugo's mother left the room and closed the door after her breathing a silent and thankful sigh of relief. She had seriously worried that the two children would not get on and she would spend the day balancing the moods of two irritating children.

Hugo heard the kitchen door close and was about to pick up one of the marshmallows, his mother had obviously bought them especially for Emma's benefit as Hugo was not normally allowed such sugary treats, when Bird reappeared still looking very worried but as soon as he saw the food he suddenly perked up and said "Ah lunch." And before Emma or Hugo had time to stop him he had eaten all the food, marshmallows included. He had eaten it so fast that you could see the lump in his throat where it lodged before slowly slipping down into his large roundish body. "Any more?" Bird asked expectantly. "NO!" Hugo almost shouted but then he remembered the extra bread roll he had filched the day before and which was sitting in his cupboard drawer. "I got this for you yesterday, it may be a bit stale now." Bird ignored and him and with one swallow it slid down his throat joining the rest of Hugo's and Emma's lunch. Hugo's stomach gave an involuntary gurgle. "You're mum's a good cook but now to business." Bird said with a flap and stretch of his wings which almost knocked Emma off the bed. One other strange thing happened, with the intake of food, bird seemed inexplicably to grow a little. A fact that was not missed by either of the children.

CHAPTER 6

The Toothfairy

Deep in the bowels of the cave Kadavera worked tirelessly to formulate herself a potion that would allow her to venture into the sunlight. She had almost exhausted all of the pathetic creatures which she used to try out her various recipes. A large pile of oddly-patterned stones lay in a heap beside the old, decaying, wooden door ready to be thrown into the sea at the first opportunity. Steam and smoke drifted above the various pots and cauldrons that littered the floor and hearth. Kadavera shuffled around, stirring and sniffing each receptacle, adding a pinch of this and a piece of that to each one. Some pots suddenly burst into brightly coloured flames as the ingredients were added almost singeing her eyebrows while others just gave an ominous belch followed by a jet of steam or noxious coloured gas. "This time, this time." she muttered to herself and with that crossed over to the remaining boxes. She prised open two of them. From one she took a large black and white rabbit that she had stolen several nights before from the hutch of one of those pathetic human children that lived not far away. The rabbit kicked and struggled, fighting to get free but the witch held on firmly to its ears and ignored the pleading squeals from the animal. As she opened the second box a tiny but piercing scream was heard. So extreme was the sound that several of the glass jars on the workbench exploded sending shards of glass and bubbling potions all over the room. "You'll pay for that!" screamed the witch. "You've ruined a month's work. I'll have to start again." With that the witch threw the rabbit back into the box and hammered down the lids. She then gave the box from where the screaming had emanated a violent kick and hissed. "I'm going make something very special for you my dear that will stop your' screaming once and for all." With that she turned, kicked the box with the back of her heal and shuffled back to her bench still hissing and cursing.

The rabbit in the one box fell on its back and breathed heavily. "Oh thank you, thank you." it said to the other box. "I really thought that my time had come. Who or what are you?" A little high pitched voice rose from the adjacent box saying, "My name is Puchy and I am a Toothfairy." "Hello," said the rabbit "My name is Thwack, but what's a Toothfairy." "Oh we never visit rabbits, because your teeth don't fall out. They just keep growing, but human children start to lose their first teeth at about six years old and when it happens they put the fallen out tooth under their pillow at night and we Toothfairies come along and take the teeth and replace it with some money." "Why do you do that?" questioned the rabbit. "Well we Toothfairies need the fallen out teeth to build our houses and it seems unfair to take the teeth and not pay for them so this is why we leave the money. Most children, as they get older, think that it's their parents who put the money under the pillow and stop doing it before we have gathered all their teeth and some children let their teeth get so rotten that they are really useless for what we need but if we stop putting the money under the pillow they stop leaving their good teeth and so we do it anyway."

"How did you get caught?" Thwack asked. "Well, I was visiting a little boy called Hugo Bennett, who lives not far from here. His father is a dentist and so his teeth were perfect and just what I wanted. He had put his tooth under his pillow, he even made it easier for me as he put it near the edge, and I was just about to exchange his tooth for a two pound coin when I saw a shadow on the window and realised that it was that old hag over there that I had been warned about. I stayed very still but she must have seen me and she materialised through the wall and grabbed me. I just had time to write a note saying "help me" when she grabbed me, put me in her sack and brought me here."

"Do you think he will help you?" asked Thwack. "I don't really know Puchy said sadly, "I am not very optimistic and he is only a small boy. I doubt that he would be able to take on Kadavera and all her spells." "Quiet!" suddenly Kadavera's voice rang out." I told you not to speak." And with that she came across to the boxes and violently kicked them apart so that neither inmate could hear each other.

"My friend Barguff said that he thought that Kadavera's cave is not far from your house here," mused Bird as he scratched his wing feathers with his foot which Hugo now noticed was like that of an eagle rather than that of an ostrich," but he couldn't tell me much more. "He was so overjoyed at escaping that he didn't pay much attention to where he was going because as it was now becoming light and gnomes must not be seen moving during daylight hours, he had to keep dodging back and forth to avoid the humans out and about at that time. He said that he was convinced a milkman had seen him move but when he came to look he fell over onto his side to make it look as if the wind had moved him and blown him over. At least the milkman seemed convinced. The only useful bit of information that Barguff did say was that the cave was very close to the sea as he could hear the waves crashing on the pebbles while he was in there."

"Well that helps to narrow it down a bit." interjected Hugo, "because if it's near here and you can hear the sea on the pebbles then that rules out Westward Ho! as the beach there is sandy so it must be this way towards Abbotsham or a bit further to Peppercombe." "What fascinating names. "Bird mused to himself. "So if we all head that way we might see something." broke in Emma. "I'm sorry I won't be able to join you," Bird said disappointedly, "but I mustn't be seen by adults as they do not understand who and what I am and they will try and capture me or even worse but I'll tell you what if you do discover something say my name out loud three times and I will come to you." "I'll never be able to remember your name. What is it Philia something or other?" said Hugo. "Oh don't worry I answer just as well to Bird." "Thank heavens for that. "sighed Emma but continued "But I thought that you could make yourself invisible?" "Oh I can." replied Bird but not for long periods, it takes a lot of energy to stay invisible and it makes me weak especially if I haven't eaten much." He looked at Hugo with a suggestive look.

"I take the hint." and with that Hugo climbed off the bed and went to see if he could find some food. "Get some for me too." whispered Emma and as she said this, Hugo was also reminded by a loud gurgle from his stomach that he had not eaten anything either since breakfast as Bird had scoffed his and Emma's lunches.

When Hugo went into the kitchen his mother looked up and asked how everything was going as it had seemed very quiet. "Oh OK, Hugo replied nonchalantly. "Anything else to eat mum? we're both still starving and something smells really good?" Hugo need not have bothered asking for just at that moment his mother was taking a tray of scones out of the oven and as the smell wafted towards Hugo his stomach gave an even louder rumble. "My word, you really are hungry." his mother said, also hearing the rumble, "I think that you had better have an extra one." "An extra two… each would be even better." Hugo purred enthusiastically.

"Alright, but that's all, I need to save some for your father when he gets in. These are his favourite. Oh and here is some jam and clotted cream to go with them." "Oh thanks mum." Hugo gushed and kissed his mum on the cheek. "That girl must come around more often. "She thought to herself. "It's certainly perked young Hugo up."

Hugo took a plate and carefully, so as not to burn his fingers on the hot delicacies, counted out six of the biggest ones he could find. On a second plate he spooned as large a portion of Devon clotted cream as he could without raising suspicion and carefully, with a plate in each hand he returned to his room with his trophies. "Look what I've got." He announced as he opened the door and both Bird and Emma gazed in amazement open mouthed. Before any one of them moved, especially Bird, Hugo firmly said. "It's two each, ONLY TWO." And with that he looked directly at Bird with a very serious face. Emma took a look at the scones and said seriously, "Did you know that if you put the jam on first and then the cream it's called a Cornish Cream Tea but if you put the cream on first and then the jam it's called a Devon Cream Tea. Or is it the other way round? It doesn't matter but each county are quite adamant that theirs is the best and that the other county has got it wrong. One thing, however, they do agree on is that you must use real clotted cream not the rubbish you get from the supermarket." "Well I didn't know that." Hugo said spraying a mouthful of cream-coated crumbs all over the bed and Bird. "I don't care what they're called, they're really good." agreed Bird. Well, the scones, jam and clotted cream all disappeared in less than a minute despite having to hold the pieces in the mouth while breathing in and out to cool them, after which everyone slumped back with a satisfied look on all their faces. Hugo took this opportunity to lick the plate so that not a crumb was wasted and the plate shone by the time he had finished. Hugo picked up the plates and took them downstairs back to the kitchen returning shortly with two large glasses of orange squash. He took a glass of squash and handed it to Emma while he picked up the other. This was the only thing from lunch that bird had not devoured and was a pleasant finale to the feast. "I wish your mum would show my mum how to cook like that." Said Emma as she slumped down on the bed letting out a big sigh of satisfaction.

"Well it's too late to do anything today so we'll start looking tomorrow." said Hugo to Bird with a little belch. "Skuze me" he said quietly and blushing a little. "If you want to?" he said turning to Emma as if it was understood that she was now part of the team. "You bet!" she exclaimed and then as an afterthought "If my mum will let me." "I'll tell you what, I'll pop down and ask mum if she can ring your mum on her mobile and see if she will let you stay over then we can make an early start in the morning and get much more ground covered." Emma's eyes lit up and she agreed that it was a great idea and besides she was getting very bored at home being by herself with just her mum who was not the best of company after her dad had been taken into hospital.

Hugo and Emma jumped off the bed and ran to the kitchen, suddenly stopping short. "Oh I'm glad you're here Emma because your mum has just phoned and she had a problem with the car and it's delayed her so much that she can't get home tonight. She asked me if you could stay the night, we have a spare room and she will pick you up tomorrow evening. She said that your father was much better and could come out of hospital so she is going to come home with him." Emma's eyes lit up. Two bits of good news at the same time. "I'll dig out some of Stephanie's night clothes that she doesn't wear any more. I'm sure that we can find something that will fit. Is that OK with you?" she said turning to Hugo who shuffled and mumbled "Spoze so." Though deep down he was thinking "Yippee! How's that for a stroke of luck."

Your father and Stephanie will be home quite soon so both of you go upstairs and get washed ready for tea. I'll give you a call when it's ready. Oh how's the game going?" "Alright they said in harmony but showing little enthusiasm in their voices.

CHAPTER 7

The Gnome Reserve

Dinner was a fairly subdued affair as far as Hugo and Emma were concerned as they didn't want to risk mentioning accidentally about Bird and the tales he had told them but this was more than made up by Stephanie who never seemed to stop talking about her day out with "Marty" and his family. They had taken a trip to Clovelly, a small fishing village built and balanced on the edge of a cliff. It was frequently used as a backdrop for films and television programmes. She made out that she had been an absolute martyr having to climb the steep street that winds through the whole village. Her mother said that she had heard how pretty it was and that she would like to go there before the end of summer. Stephanie then, between mouthfuls of tinned peaches and ice cream, described how on the return journey they had gone to a really quaint little place called the Gnome Reserve where you were asked to wear a little gnome's hat as you went round so that you did not upset the gnomes. Hugo and Emma suddenly sat up and bombarded Stephanie with questions about who and what she saw. Stephanie was taken aback with the sudden interest shown in her day by her brother and friend but now appearing as the centre of attention she thought and tried to describe as many details as she could remember. Hugo's father noticed the young pair's interest and asked why they were so interested in the Gnome Reserve. "Oh! No reason in particular. Our teacher mentioned it while we were at school." He lied. Emma reinforced the untruth by enthusiastically agreeing with him. Both parents looked at each other quizzically. The apparent bonding of the two children was not what they had expected but they were not going to argue with this bonus.

The two young children were still busily engaged in conversation with Stephanie, who was lapping up being the centre of attention, when Mr Bennett, who was now sat down in his favourite chair reading the local newspaper, suddenly said. "I see that they have postponed that Time Team excavation. It seems that while they were setting up, all their electrical equipment failed for no apparent reason and they have had to send off to some specialist company for replacements. They blamed it on the Gremlins so they have rescheduled it for the 25nd of August and to finish on the 28th. Hugo and Emma suddenly stopped talking to Stephanie and looked at each other open-mouthed.

Hugo's mother used the lull in the conversation to ask if the children had any plans for the next day so that she would know how to plan hers. Stephanie proudly announced that Marty's mother was going to Exeter to "engage in some retail therapy" as she put it and that she had invited Stephanie along with her. Marty was spending the day playing horrible football and would not be coming. Mrs Bennett felt a little jealous and upset for she had planned to go herself in a couple of days and surprise Stephanie but now that had put that idea on the back burner. Hugo piped up," Emma said that she knew a fantastic part of the old railway track near Westward Ho! that was the perfect spot for a picnic so we thought that, if you can make us a packed lunch, please mum, we could take Jake and explore it." Emma looked surprised because she had said nothing of the kind but quickly understood why Hugo had suggested it. His mother looked at his father to ensure approval and then she said "Well that's alright then but I want you home before four and take my mobile phone with you just in case. The two children smiled at each other and proceeded to sit down in front of the television to watch another repeat of "The A -Team". Since it was a rerun Hugo knew exactly what would happen but he still enjoyed watching it, especially how they seemingly made fantastic machines out of apparently nothing and went on to capture all the baddies. Hugo always made the comment that despite hundreds of shots being fired in every episode no one was ever killed or seriously injured. While their backs were turned, Mr Bennett whispered to his wife. "It's a good job they're not a few years older." Mrs Bennett took his meaning, blushed, smiled and then gave him a disapproving stare.

At eight o'clock Mrs Bennett told Hugo and Emma that it was time for bed. Both children gave a moan and asked why was it that Stephanie was allowed to stay up later. "Because she's older." came back the standard reply. "If you come with me Emma, I'll show you where your room is and we will see if we can dig out some pyjamas for you." She went on. "I have left you a new toothbrush and some toothpaste in the bathroom but if you need anything else then let me know."

With that she turned and started to go up the stairs followed by Emma and a still complaining Hugo. He thought that Bird might be in his room when he opened the door but there was no sign and so he changed into his pyjamas, went to the bathroom and brushed his teeth. He looked closely at the space left by his missing tooth and was surprised to see that he could just start to see the first signs of the new one coming into its place, just like his dad had said. "that's great he thought to himself." For although most of the children in his class were missing at least one tooth he still felt a little embarrassed when he smiled and he couldn't wait for the new one to grow back.

He went back to his room going over in his mind about spending the day with Emma, who, for a girl, wasn't too bad. He pondered over the second visit of Bird, the explanation by Stephanie all about the Gnome Reserve, the news that the Time Team programme had been postponed and was to be rescheduled for the 25th of August. He wondered if this was significant and then where and what he might find on his expedition with Emma along the old railway track as they tried to find the cave mentioned by the gnome called Barguff. He didn't know when he fell asleep but the next thing he knew was Jake jumping onto his bed with the morning sunlight streaming through his window.

CHAPTER 8

The Cave

Hugo was the first to get up that morning and so he washed, cleaned his teeth, dressed and went downstairs. Jake kept whimpering and getting under Hugo's feet as he tried to persuade him to feed him. Finally Hugo succumbed and picking up Jake's bowl he filled it with a good helping of Chum and as he put it down for the expectant dog he said. "I've given you extra today, we've got a lot of walking ahead of us." And then went to get his own breakfast leaving Jake with his head buried in his bowl and his tail wagging wildly. Hugo looked into the cupboard for some Cheerios but then remembered that Bird had devoured the lot but then suddenly his eyes lit up for there on the shelf was a big box of Sugar Puffs, Hugo's most favourite cereal. His mother had specially bought them since Emma was staying and for once had disobeyed the advice of her husband. Hugo was unsure whether to break into this box of forbidden fruit but "what the hell." He thought and poured himself a large bowlful. He was halfway through eating them when his parents came down to breakfast and his father also grabbed the Sugar Puffs and almost filled his bowl. Hugo looked at him and was about to admonish him and remind him of what he always said when his dad looked at his mother and then at Hugo and said "Do what I say not what I do." and then smiled broadly.

It was over an hour before Stephanie and Emma rose and breakfasted, all indulging in the rare treat of the Sugar Puffs to the extent that the new box was almost empty by the time everyone had taken their share. "I should of hidden them." thought Hugo. His mother busied herself making sandwiches for the packed lunches, only stopping to answer the door and greeting Mrs Edmunds who had called to pick up Stephanie for their shopping trip. She put the food in a small rucksack together with a couple of bottles of fruit juice, a large bottle of water, both for the children and Jake, two of the scones she had cooked the previous day already loaded with a thick layer of jam and clotted cream, a couple of doggy chews for Jake as well as some polythene bags" in case of need", again for Jake and finally a small plastic bowl for the dog to drink from. She buckled the top of the bag and then turning to both children she said," Now I'm putting my mobile in the very front pocket of the bag. I do not expect that you will need it but it is there for emergencies only. I have left it switched on in case I need to contact you. Do you both understand?" Both children nodded their heads and motioned towards the door. "Oh, I forgot. Here's some money in case you need it or fancy an ice cream or something." "Oh thanks mum." Hugo replied as Mrs Bennett passed over two two-pound coins which he looked at, smiled and then put the coins in his trouser pocket. "Now remember what I said, behave yourselves and don't get into any trouble and be back by four o'clock at the latest or there will be trouble." reiterated Mrs Bennett.

Hugo picked up the rucksack positioned it over his shoulders, making sure all the straps were tight, fastened the leash onto Jakes collar, who immediately knew that he was going for a walk and headed straight for the door, then kissing his mother on the cheek, which made him blush with Emma watching, the two children opened the door and went out to begin their adventure of "find the cave".

The initial excitement spurred them on along the old railway track that led to Abbotsham Cliffs and beyond with Jake frequently racing ahead and then doubling back, constantly wagging his bushy tail but after about half an hour of walking Hugo stopped and turned around several times. "What's wrong?" enquired Emma. "I don't really know what we are looking for, do you? If we keep walking at this pace we might miss something so I suggest that we slow down a bit and keep our eyed peeled to see if we can find any clues like the trackers do on the tele." "Good idea." Emma replied and so they continued on but at a much slower pace glancing left and right as they went along.

They'd been going for over an hour and a half and seen nothing that might be construed as significant when Hugo, or rather his stomach, decided that it was time to take a break and enjoy some of the picnic that his mother had prepared. Emma did not need any prompting to stop as it was obvious that the initial enthusiasm for the hunt was rapidly beginning to wear off on both of them. So they found suitable spot and sat down on a small hillock. Hugo took off the rucksack and started to unpack it. Since Jake's bowl came out first Hugo decided to give him his drink first. Jake was obviously thirsty as, with noisy lapping, he quickly drained it forcing Hugo to stop unwrapping their own lunches to fill the bowl again. At the same time he threw Jake a doggy chew which he attacked without hesitation. Emma and Hugo demolished the sandwiches as eagerly as Jake had his chew then they started on the scones that Mrs Bennett had made. They ate these more slowly, wanting to savour every mouthful.

Hugo picked up a stick lying by his side and threw it so that Jake could run, chase and retrieve it. The dog did this about six times when Hugo, tiring of throwing it, rolled over and started to stand. As he did so he put his hand on a small roundish rock with a faint zigzag pattern on it. He stopped rolling and sat back down picking up the stone as he did so. "Hey look at this?" he almost shouted to Emma. "it's just like the one Bird was in but smaller. Remember what Bird said about the witch getting rid of the dead bodies from her experiments. This could be one of them and that means," Hugo did not have time to finish as Emma screamed out with excitement. "The cave must be nearby. Let's have a good look to see if we can find anymore stones and they may lead us to the cave." The two children turned onto their hands and knees and began to comb the area around where they had been sitting. Jake thought that they were playing with him and jumped and barked around them. A few minutes went by when Emma suddenly screamed out. "Found one." and held up a small grey round rock about the size of an egg but with a distinctive zigzag pattern around its periphery. "Great" shouted Hugo "keep looking." For over an hour they searched around on their hands and knees with the occasional interruption of "I've found another." Suddenly Emma shouted "I've found it, I've found it. Come quickly." Hugo immediately stood up and raced to where Emma was standing and pointing to a small crack in the edge of the cliff which was pretty insignificant except that very fine wisps of smoke and steam were emerging, like a ghost materialising. The vapours seemed to change colour and smelled terrible. "This is definitely the place" Hugo said, "but how do we get in? The crack's too small for us. It might be OK for a gnome but we will never squeeze through that space. And it's far too dark for me to see inside." "Wait!" exclaimed Emma and ran back to where the rucksack lay. Pushing Jake away, who thought he was going to get another chew she rummaged in the rucksack and announced, "Got it." And raced back to where Hugo was standing. "What on earth do you want that for? Going to phone for some help?" Emma held up the mobile phone that Mrs Bennett had packed "in case of emergency" "Watch!" she said and switched the phone on so that the dial lit up. "We can use this like a torch." She said proudly and Hugo responded with "Brilliant." He wished that he had thought of it. They pointed the phone into the cave at arms-length, waving to and fro to see if they could see what was inside. As Hugo withdrew the phone he glanced at the dial which displayed a clock. "Crumbs, look at the time. We promised that we'd be back by four. We'll never make it even if we run!" He exclaimed. "I know, I'll ring mum on the phone to tell her that we'll be a bit late but we'll have to go now." The two children rose from their knees, ran to the rucksack, threw everything inside, not noticing that Jake's bowl still had some water left in it so that it made the whole of the inside of the rucksack wet. "Don't forget the stones." Emma shouted to Hugo. "They're in the bottom." he shouted back and with that he hoisted the bag back onto his back. "I'll just phone Mum." he shouted and dialled the number. His mother answered after a small delay and Hugo explained that they would be a bit late home as they had walked father than they had planned and hadn't noticed the time. Hugo's mother was relieved that her son had had the common sense to phone her explaining that he would be late but warned him not to be too late as Emma's mother was coming to pick her up. Hugo repacked the phone but then took it out again realising that the pocket in the rucksack where he had put it was wet from Jake's water so he pushed it into his trouser pocket. They started back at a fast pace but had not gone far when Hugo stopped and said that they had better mark the place where the cave was so that they could easily find it again so they turned and rushed back. Look around Hugo noticed some white stones. "That's quartz." explained Emma. "I know." Replied Hugo but admitted to himself that he had no idea what the stones were made of. "See if you can find a few more and we can use them as a marker. It took only a few minutes to find the stones and make a small cairn by the side of the track. With this done they set off again. At first they talked wildly about what they had found and what the next stage could be. They both agreed that their first priority was to tell Bird and show him the stones, which Hugo noticed, like the time he took Bird's stone home with him, that they were much heavier than their size suggested. They hadn't travelled more than half way home when all talking stopped as they both panted with the effort of the forced march.

It was 4.45 when they finally opened the door to Hugo's house. His mother rushed up to them asking if they were alright. Seeing that they were she motioned them into the kitchen where she had prepared a meal of Tuna salad with new boiled potatoes and rhubarb crumble with thick custard for pudding. It was obvious that Hugo was not a great fan of the salad but there was no trace of the pudding by the time he had finished. Meanwhile Jake was tucking into a large bowl of Chum as if he had never been fed. Mrs Bennett left the room while they were eating and when she came back she explained to Emma that her mother had phoned and that she would be picking her up at six. In the meantime while she was waiting she could watch television. However, much to her surprise Emma asked if they could go up to Hugo's room to finish the game on the computer. This surprised even Hugo but Emma explained that she had won the last race and wanted to give Hugo a chance of getting his own back. She gave Hugo a wink and so he went along with the plan but could not understand what her real motives were.

As soon as the door to Hugo's bedroom was shut she turned to him, put a finger up to her lips to tell him to keep quiet and then she said "Bird. Bird. Bird." A few moments elapsed during which Hugo wondered what on earth she was doing and then the penny dropped. He had forgotten that Bird had said that if they ever needed him all they had to do was to say his name, or at least the name of Bird, out loud three times and he would come. By the time this had dawned on him the wall of his bedroom had begun to shimmer and Bird appeared looking a little worried. "What's up with you two?" he asked inquisitively and they both tried to answer him at the same time. "One at a time." he shouted, though quietly so that no one downstairs would hear. They both immediately stopped talking but then Emma took up the tale. She explained about the walk, finding the stones, which by now Hugo was dragging out of the still wet rucksack and putting on the bed in front of Bird. She went on about finding the crack in the cliff face and how they tried to see what was inside but couldn't see despite trying to use the phone as a torch.

Bird sat intently throughout the telling of the adventure the two had had but when Emma finally stopped, a little out of breath from reliving all the excitement Bird gave them a very stern look and said that had been very silly searching for the cave, let alone having found it, because the witch was very evil and had they been caught they would almost certainly been killed and most unpleasantly too he emphasised. He sat and thought carefully for several minutes then asked the children where exactly they had found the cave. They explained exactly where they had discovered it and described the small cairn of white quartz stones that they had left to identify the spot. Bird congratulated them on their foresight but warned them that under no circumstances were they to ever go there again and never try entering the cave. The consequences could by dire.

At that point Mrs Bennett's voice echoed up the stairs. "Emma. Your mother is here." and with that Bird once again melted into nothing.

Emma got up ready to go but just before she opened the door of Hugo's bedroom she whispered. "Don't forget to let me know what happens, here's my mobile number." With that she picked up a small scrap of paper that was lying on Hugo's desk and wrote down her number. "Have you got your own mobile phone?" he asked with surprise. "My parents said that I was still too young and since they are banned at school it would be a waste of money me having one." "Mine thought that too up until recently but what with dad being ill and mum having to travel down to Exeter every day to work she thought that I needed one in case of emergencies." "Oh I see." Said Hugo and left it at that but deep down he felt a little left out, after all many of his classmates had them and took them to school despite the ban. They all used to hide around the corners at playtime and play with the games on the phones. However, one small thing that did compensate a little was that there was a lot of jealousy amongst the "phonies" as they were referred to as to having the most up to date model or the latest game. Hugo gave a little chuckle to himself thinking that if he had a phone he'd be keeping up with the Jones's, the Emma Jones's.

When they reached the kitchen Emma's mother was sitting having a cup of tea with Hugo's mum. "Hi you old scamp." she said to Emma getting up and giving her daughter a big hug and kiss on the cheek. "Where's dad?" Emma enquired looking around to see if he was there. "Oh! I'm sorry kitten but he was just getting ready to leave when the doctor in charge of his case said that they needed to do a few more test on him before they could give him the all clear, so he is staying at the hospital for another two days. It was a wasted journey in one way but it was good to see him and he looks much better. He sends his love. I have to go back up again in three days to bring him back so Mrs Bennett here has kindly volunteered to let you stay again if that's alright with you and this young man here doesn't mind putting up with you for another day." Mrs Bennett looked at Hugo enquiringly without saying anything but Hugo understood the look and mumbled, "Spoze so" trying his best not to look too pleased at the prospect of spending another day with his new friend. Emma gave a similar response but was equally overjoyed at being able to continue the adventure and find out what was going to happen with the witch and Bird.

The two days by himself seemed to drag now that he had become used to having company. Stephanie seemed even more obnoxious than ever, taunting at every opportunity saying "Where's your girlfriend then? Or, Are you missing your girlfriend?" "At least she isn't spotty like someone I know." he retorted on one occasion which made Stephanie scream and chase him around the table. She had been brushing her hair and in a rage she threw the hair brush at him narrowly missing the large mirror. The commotion brought Jake in on the act and he jumped around barking and wagging his tail furiously. Mrs Bennett stormed in from the kitchen. "Both of you go to your rooms. Immediately! " Hugo tried to explain that it was Stephanie's fault but Mrs Bennett repeated "NOW!" It was no good arguing and the two children slouched up the stairs together elbowing each other as they went and muttering oaths at each other until they finally separated into their respective rooms. Hugo threw himself down onto his bed still muttering curses at his sister and remained there until his mother called him down for tea. While his mother and father happily discussed the events of the day Hugo and Stephanie sat in absolute silence throwing daggers at each other from their eyes.

CHAPTER 9

Birds Mistake

Bird had been quite worried at the irresponsibility of the two young children and felt that he was to blame and that he had not stressed to them the dangers involved in going after Kadavera. To avoid any further risk he decided to sort out the problem himself, once and for all. At first light the day after his meeting with Hugo and Emma he set off, in his invisible state to ensure he wasn't seen by an adult human, along the old railway track to the site where the children had said they found the cave.

Surprisingly, the instructions that Emma had given him as to the whereabouts of the cave were very accurate and quickly identified the quartz stone cairn marker. He sniffed the air and although he could not see any smoke or fumes coming out of the small crack in the cliff face he could still smell the sulphurous overtones around the surrounding rocks. He cautiously peered into the crack and listened very intently. Nothing could be heard except the crashing of the waves on the rocks immediately below him. Using his power of disembodiment he squeezed through the opening and found himself in a small irregular passageway. To save energy he allowed himself to return to normal visibility and he shook his feathers to straighten them out after the squeeze. The walls were very rough and tool marks could be seen where the stone had been chiselled out by people in the past, probably seeking iron ore which was once mined in this area. The tunnel was very dark with the only light coming from the open crack in the cliff. As Bird inched his way down, the light gradually diminished until darkness was total. All Bird could do was to stretch his wings so that he could sense the sides of the tunnel and carefully feel with each foot every inch of the floor. The putrid air he smelt before he entered the tunnel became more and more intense. He had to fight to stop himself coughing as he did not wish to give away his presence, just in case. For several minutes he eased his way along the tunnel till, as his eyes adapted to the darkness, he saw, far off in the distance, a pinpoint of light. As he continued to move forward the point of light slowly became bigger and bigger until Bird could see that the end of the tunnel opened out into a large cavern.

He tiptoed up to the entrance to the cave, which was quite difficult when your feet are like eagle claws, but he did not want them to make any scraping noises on the hard floor. He slowly put his head around the edge of the entrance. The only illumination was from a few soot-encrusted oil lamps fixed to the walls, a few sputtering candles on a central table, which was covered by a complete mish-mash of pots, old tin cans, an assortment of jam jars, some empty and some full of very dubious contents plus some small glass vials also containing potions some of which actually seemed to glow. Against one wall was a large fire topped by a huge caldron from which emanated multi-coloured smoke and an absolutely nauseating smell. Small stalactites hung from the roof, dripping water, making the whole cave echo to the tiny splashes, however, they were no longer a pristine cream colour as those usually seen in pictures. Instead they were thickly encrusted with soot with only streaks of the underlying stone seen where the water had washed away the deposits.

Bird strained his eyes to try and see into the darkest recesses of the cave to see if he could detect any signs of life or movement, especially any that might show the presence of Kadavera. He could see nothing but did notice a faint sobbing emanating from the depths of a hollow cut into the far wall. Thinking that caution was the best course of action he made himself invisible, despite feeling decidedly peckish, and entered the main body of the cave. He kept to the walls trying to keep as silent as he could. He even made a point of controlling his breathing so that he made as little noise as possible. As he approached the far corner he nearly hit over a large pot that was perched on the edge of a low shelf but he managed to catch it before it hit the ground. Now, deep inside the cave, the stench of the various smoking potions was really getting to his throat and he frequently had to fight to stop himself coughing. He finally reached the dark recess from where he had heard the faint crying. It was so dark here that it was almost impossible to see anything. All he could make out were some small wooden boxes but who or what they contained was anybody's guess. All he could be sure of was that there was something alive inside.

Looking all around him to make sure that he was safe and that no one could see him he quietly whispered, "Hello. Is there anybody there?" The crying stopped immediately and other than the faint dripping of the water from the stalactites, there was complete silence. Bird again looked around to ensure that he was not being observed and then repeated. "Hello. Is there anybody there?" A faint high pitched squeaky voice suddenly whispered back, "Hello. Who's there?" "My name is Phila…." Bird stopped, remembering the difficulty Hugo had had pronouncing his name let alone remembering it. "Just call me Bird." he continued as quietly as he could. Who are you?" "I'm Puchy the Toothfairy, "came back a small voice." That awful witch Kadavera captured me a few days ago as I was trying to exchange a tooth for a little boy called Hugo Bennett. I did manage to leave a little note asking for help but I doubt that he ever saw it or if he did, did not understand what was going on." "Oh he read it alright." Bird whispered, "That's why I'm here now." "Where are you anyway?" cried the small voice. "I can't see you." Bird suddenly realised that he was still invisible and so, not wanting to give the Toothfairy any further distress he switched back to being normal again. His stomach gurgled in response. As he materialised the small voice said "You really are a bird…of sorts." "Well thank you very much. What did you expect with a name like mine an elephant?" "Well there are certain similarities." chuckled the Toothfairy looking at Bird's ears. "Well that's a long story," he replied feeling a little self-conscious. Let's get you out of here." And with that Bird held onto the crate and as noiselessly as he could started to prise the lid off the top, which was not as easy as it sounds as he only had wings not hands and fingers. Eventually with a creaking and splintering of wood the lid gave way. Bird carefully put his wing into the inside of the crate and helped the small fairy out and onto the floor. Although the light was exceedingly dim Bird could make out a small petite figure about fifteen centimetres tall wearing a sparkling silver-coloured dress, which had lost a lot of its sparkle due to the dirt that now coated it. She also had a pair of gossamer-thin wings sprouting from her back. "You look just like the fairies you see in story books except that you have black hair rather than "fine golden locks"." "What did you expect?" The fairy retorted indignantly, shaking her hair and ruffling her wings. "Where do you think that the story- tellers got their ideas from and my hair is golden but having spent several days in that dirty old box it needs a good wash." "I'm terribly sorry." Bird apologised, a little sheepishly, having been put in his place in no uncertain terms. "Let's get you out of here." "Oh wait," the Toothfairy cried out quietly "don't forget Thwack." "Thwack?" Bird said quizzically. "Yes my friend Thwack, he's a rabbit, and he's trapped in that other box over there. Kadavera has been using us and lots of other animals for her experiments to allow her to roam around in the daylight so that she can fulfil her plans to get revenge on some people who did something very bad to her family many years ago. Thwack was nearly killed yesterday had I not screamed and broken some of the witch's jars containing her potions. She was going to try her latest concoction out on him. I think that she has almost perfected the recipe and I don't think it will be long before she succeeds." "Not if I have my way she won't" Bird said but then from behind him came a gravelly voice that said "Don't you believe it." and before he had realised it a large heavy net had been thrown over him anchoring him to the ground.

"Quick run!" Bird screamed at the Toothfairy "Go! and see Hugo and tell him." But he never had the chance to finish his sentence which was to have been "NOT to come looking for him." The little fairy did not need a second telling and in a combination of skips, jumps and fluttering of her wings she danced and skittered across the floor avoiding the various objects being hurled at her by the witch. The racket had disturbed Thwack in his crate and he stood up as best he could and shouted! "Go fairy GO!" beating his foot on the floor of the box as loudly as he could. The small figure flitted around the cave until she found the entrance to the tunnel and with a final turn of her head to see what was happening she rushed down the tunnel towards daylight and freedom.

"Welcome back." The old witch cackled. "We meet again my feathery friend. I thought that I'd seen the last of you but now that you're here you can help me with some more of my little…um…cocktails." Her sudden hysterical laugh echoed around the cave and reverberated from the walls. Bird began to feel a little afraid but did not want Kadavera to know this so he announced loudly. "Well thank you, you old crone. Nice to see you again too. I like what you've done with the cave while I've been away, quite homely. By the way what's for lunch? I'm starving." Kadavera laughed sarcastically and looking down at the boxes sneeringly and said "Rabbit stew." Thwack suddenly stopped beating his foot on the bottom of the crate and cowered in the corner on the box as he knew that the old witch was not joking. Snatch, the cat-like animal she kept as a pet curled round her legs making a sort of chattering noise with its mouth and eyeing Bird hungrily.

Bird wriggled and wiggled to try to free himself but he knew that it was no good and for good measure Kadavera was piling stones around the edges of the net to hold it down to prevent him escaping. "Now stay there and enjoy the view…while you can… I have a few little jobs to do but don't worry I'll be back quite soon and then we'll see about…. lunch!" With that, she looked down at the crate containing Thwack, who was now trembling, gave Bird an almighty kick then turned and disappeared into the gloom of the cave. "Whwhwhat we going to do?" came a frightened voice from Thwack's box. "I don't know exactly" Bird replied pensively, "But I'm sure we'll think of something." He lowered his head onto the ground and thought to himself "What are we going to do? Getting captured was not in his plan and now having done so was a big mistake

CHAPTER 10

Revenge

H ugo woke up on the second day after his adventure with Emma and looked out of the window. The sky was overcast and looked as if it might rain. He washed, cleaned his teeth and returned to his room to dig out some clothes to wear. When he went downstairs to the kitchen his father was already sat at the table eating some toast and watching the local news on the television. Hugo sat down to eat his bowl of the remaining Sugar Puffs, he wanted to make sure that he got his fair share before the rest of the family demolished what was left. His ears pricked when he heard on the news that they were planning to film the Time Team programme again following the problems they had had before and that they had agreed that the land owner, a Dr Richard Benson, who was distantly related to the infamous judge and who had mysteriously died there, would be allowed to cut the first sod of earth over, what was thought to be, the very room where the judge had died a most hideous death. The interviewer was talking to one of the presenters of the programme and asked him jokingly if he was worried by the fact that the earlier delay to the programme had now meant that they would be filming on the very anniversary of the killing. The presenter laughed and said that they had already had their share of Gremlins and one more would not make any difference. The television programme then skipped to another item on battery farming.

Hugo became so engrossed in the programme that his spoon missed his mouth and a spoonful of Puffs and milk dribbled down his shirt. "Messy pig!" Stephanie shouted as she came into the room and saw what had happened. "Get lost!" Hugo retorted spraying even more Sugar Puffs and milk over the table. Mr Bennett looked up and glowered at them and they both fell silent. Hugo grabbed a napkin and brushed down his shirt and table cloth as best he could to get rid of the scattered cereal. The television programme ended with a weather report. Hugo was interested to see what the weather was going to be like because he wanted to go back to the cave entrance but this time with a small hammer to try to make it a bit bigger so that he might get in through the gap. If it was going to be fine then he would go but if it was going to rain then he'd be stuck indoors with nothing to do and no one to do it with. The weather reporter was quite excited because he said that they expected some very unusual weather today. There was a front of high pressure, whatever that was, moving from the South and it was bringing with it the remains of a large sand storm that had been raging in the Sahara desert for the last few days. It might mean that some of the dust may be driven over England, especially the South and South Western regions and they were warning people not to put their washing out and to keep their widows closed if the dust cloud did materialise.

"Looks like I'll be staying in then." Hugo moaned to himself.

"Let's get all the geophys done first" the director said to the gathering of presenters and technicians and then we can start filming the outer trenches and get the borders of the building mapped out and then in the afternoon we can film this bod cutting the turf over what should be the study of this bloody judge." The crew gave a little chuckle. "What's he going to use to cut the first turf?" someone asked, "a spade or a pick axe." "Naw, he's a posh blighter and doesn't want to get his hands dirty," mocked the director "so he's using our JCB digger." "Well I hope he knows how to use it 'cos they can be bloody temperamental!" exclaimed a voice from the back which turned out to be the driver of the JCB. "He says that he's an expert and if he isn't well that's his hard luck." announced the director. "Now get on with it, we've got a programme to make and we've only got three days to do it in." He turned to the presenter and they both grinned and walked away to do their various bits.

Hugo's father finished watching the television and then turned to his son and asked if he fancied going to Bideford to watch the filming of the Time Team programme. He said that his mum would like to go as she was very keen on the programme and since the weather did not look promising to do anything else, it might be a good day out. He might even be able to get the presenters autograph. That would be good to show all the kids when he went back to school. Hugo's eyes lit up and immediately started to rush upstairs to change his milk sodden shirt. "Don't forget your camera." His father called after him. "What about you Steph, want to come?" "No thanks dad." she replied emphatically "can't stand the programme. I don't know what mum sees in it. All they do is dig up bits of odd looking stones and swear it's from this or that century. It's a load of old rubbish if you ask me. I'll stay in and watch the tele. This afternoon I've arranged to meet one of my friends and we're going round to her place." Her father smiled and said "OK but if you change your mind let us know and we'll come and pick you up." With that Stephanie picked up her empty breakfast bowl, took it into the kitchen, put it into the dishwasher and went up to her room.

At ten thirty Hugo and his parents piled into his dad's Volvo and headed off for the short journey to Bideford. Many of the car parks were full and they had to park some distance from where the filming was taking place. The whole of the area was cordoned off with barriers and plastic tape which warned "Do Not Cross!" The family could see the activity in the far distance but the figures were so far away that they could not see very much. Hugo's dad lifted him onto his shoulders to see if that would improve his view but it did not. A workman went passed wearing a bright Hi Viz jacket with CREW stencilled on the back. "Excuse me?" said Hugo's mother, "are they likely to be working anywhere closer." The workman stopped and turned to face her and said "Oh! Yes mam. If you come back this afternoon they've got this big wig coming over to dig the first turf from over the top of, what they think may be, the judge's study. This will be only about 30 metres from where you are now. You should get a good view. Come early though 'cos they're expecting a lot of people, what with the press and everything." With that he smiled, touched his forehead and carried on walking. "Right lets go and have a coffee while we're waiting and we can come back later and see if we have better luck." proclaimed Mr Bennett. With that they about turned and left the dig to find a suitable café where they could relax and wait until the activity started.

Bird lay quietly thinking for what must have been an hour when a shuffling noise broke the silence and Kadavera came into view. "Having fun?" she gloated when she saw Bird looking at her and gave a little cackle. She went over to the box where Thwack the rabbit was still cowering. She prised open the lid and pulled out the shaking and trembling rabbit by his ears. He waved his legs fiercely trying to escape but she held on firmly. "We've got some unfinished business my furry friend and this time you haven't got that pesky little bitch of a fairy to get you out of it." Thwack redoubled his efforts to escape but all that he managed to do was to make one of his ears bleed. The witch turned and took the struggling rabbit over to her bench where she tied his legs and then his body to the table to stop him moving.

From the end of the bench she picked up a small glass tube filled with an iridescent green liquid. She also picked up a small stick which she forced between the whimpering rabbits jaws and then slowly and carefully she trickled the green liquid into the mouth of the catatonic animal. The witch stood back to watch the fruits of her labour. At first the animal just coughed and spluttered but then began to shake and convulse. Had it not been for the bonds tying it to the table the poor rabbit would have thrown itself onto the floor. Suddenly it lay quite still. The witch came close to it and bent over to poke the petrified animal. A small flash of light issued from around her neck which caught Bird's eye. It was a small necklace carrying a small gold locket. Although Bird could not make it out very clearly it seemed to have a letter engraved on its front. He thought it looked like an "M" but he could have been mistaken because it was only a fleeting glance and then it disappeared again into her clothing. "That's weird?" Bird thought, "that seems a very unusual object for a witch to wear. It must have some special meaning. I must try and get a better look. If I get the chance." he added as an after-thought.

The witch gazed at the immobile animal lying in front of her for several minutes watching the sand percolate down the inside of a large hourglass situated just above the rabbit's head. As the last grains fell into the bottom container she went to the end of her bench and picked up another small glass tube in her dirty-yellow bony fingers. Again a small flash of light reflected from the sputtering candle but this time not from a necklace but a large gold ring on the ring finger of her right hand. In the centre of the ring was a large bright green stone which seemed to give off an eerie glow. "This is most interesting." Bird thought to himself. "I did not realise that even witches were interested in jewellery."

Kadavera carried the tube, this time containing a frothy blue liquid from which smoke was rising, over to the apparently dead rabbit and began to slowly pour the smoking liquid into its, now unresisting, mouth. She stood back, turned the hourglass and waited. Nothing seemed to happen for several minutes but then the body began to slowly move and it could be seen to be breathing. Suddenly it gave an explosive cough and splutter and its eyes flicked open. The still hooded black figure rapidly began to untie the knots of the cords that held the rabbit to the table and from around its feet. She was obviously excited for she was giggling and her bony fingers were trembling. She finally took a long length of string and tied it roughly around the neck of poor Thwack who though still alive was certainly not looking his best.

"And now for the final test." she almost sang. "Daylight, Let's see if you can live in daylight?" With that, she gathered the rabbit up into her arms and raced towards the tunnel that led to the outside and daylight. Minutes went by during which, all that could be heard was the dripping of the water from the ceiling and the echo of the shuffle of Kadavera as she travelled further and further along the tunnel. Now, there was silence.

An ear splitting scream suddenly arose and it echoed down the tunnel which acted as a megaphone making the whole cave vibrate. It was followed by the joyous shouting of "I've done it. I've done it. I've done it." Snatch, her pet animal, who had been curled up sleeping in some dark corner gave a violent yowl and ran as far away as he could from the noise hissing and spitting as it went. The scuffling began again but this time growing louder as the joyous witch almost skipped back down the tunnel. "After all these years and years I've finally done it. I can move about in the daylight without dying."

She emerged from the tunnel almost with a smile on her face, exposing the yellow-brown stumps that had once been teeth. As she passed Bird she kicked him hard and said "Got you now. Nobody can stop me. Now I can get my revenge." She threw the bedraggled rabbit, still with the string around its neck back into the box and banged the lid shut. She then went back to her bench still singing to herself. "I've done it, I've done it. I've really done it."

"What's happened?" Bird asked the recovering rabbit. "Well." coughed the still recovering rabbit "when Kadavera first became a witch she was brought back from the dead but the potions that she was given only kept her alive while she remained in the dark. If she ever went out into daylight she would die and never be able to live again. The first potion she gave me just now was the same one that she was given to bring her back from the dead but the second one was the one she has been trying to develop ever since that will allow her to exist in daylight so that she can get revenge on the people that murdered her in the first place." "Why did she need you?" asked Bird. "Well after she had given me the second potion she took me to the end of the tunnel and threw me out into the daylight to see if I would survive. The fact that I did proved that her potion worked so she hauled me back into the tunnel using this string around my neck and the rest you know about. I think that now she's making some more of the second potion so that she can take it herself and go into the daylight."

Sure enough Thwack was right and as Kadavera busied herself making the potion she muttered oaths and curses and recited the terrible things she was going to do to "Those murderers."

Hours passed until finally there was a scream of excitement and the old witch held up a vial of the frothy blue smoking liquid to the candle light and with a gesture of taking a toast she threw the mixture into her mouth and loudly swallowed. For several minutes nothing happened and even Kadavera started to worry that it was not working when suddenly she gave a piecing scream and fell on the floor convulsing. Slowly she calmed down until she was quite still. She lay motionless for several minutes but then quietly she began to stir. She moved her fingers, then her hands. Her arms lifted from the floor and she carefully twisted until she was face down. Inch by inch she tucked her limbs under her body and pushed up until she was kneeling. Then with what seemed a great effort she stood and stretched. She felt all around her body with her bony hands to make sure everything was where it was supposed to be and then with a tremendous yell she screamed "YES! YES! YES! I've really done it." She even appeared to dance a little jig in triumph. "Now I'm going to get you!" she exclaimed and with that she pulled her ragged cloak around her and almost ran towards and into the tunnel until nothing could be heard but the drip, drip, drip, of the water from the dirty black stalactites on the roof.

The café where they had a drink overlooked the quay at Bideford and Hugo was fascinated to watch the large boat moored up being loaded with large tree trunks that were being delivered to the quay by a succession of lorry's. His father ordered a Cappuccino and his mother an Earl Grey tea. Hugo could not make up his mind but eventually settled on a banana milkshake. His father took a sip out of his drink and then pushed his face toward Hugo. All around his dad's mouth was a big moustache of foam. He poked out his tongue and licked all around his mouth with a big slurp which made Hugo and his father laugh. His mother just looked and shook her head. His father's coffee came with a small biscuit and Hugo made a point of showing his dad that he had noticed it till eventually he relented and pushed it over to Hugo. It disappeared without trace within seconds as Hugo licked his lips. "Right let's go and see what we can see." his father said as Mrs Bennett finally pushed her empty cup away from her and replaced all the cups back on the tray and took them back to the counter. Five minutes later they were back standing where they had positioned themselves before but the workman had been right, there were certainly far more people here now and several of them had large cameras and sound recording equipment with funny microphones that looked like dead cats on the end of long poles. The Time Team presenters and crew were now only about 100 meters away and they could see them studying various laptop computers and charts frequently pointing in various directions. The same workman as before walked passed again and looking round he commented "Back again I see." and then continued on his way.

The wind was beginning to pick up and the sky becoming overcast, taking on a reddish hue. "It looks like we may get that sand storm they mentioned on the weather forecast" Mr Bennett said and he looked up into the air. Thick clouds were rolling in from a southerly direction and the flag on some buildings nearby started to flap and crack in the increasing wind. Just then a big black Mercedes Benz with the number plate RB1 pulled up at the entrance to the site and the driver got out and opened the back door. A large man emerged wearing a smart grey suit. He ducked under the plastic tape which was held up for him by the driver and went up to the director with his hand outstretched. The director shook it and then introduced the man to the programme presenters and senior members of the production crew. The man was escorted to a part of the site, about 30 meters from where Hugo and his parents were standing, to where a large yellow JCB stood. The director shouted some instructions to some of the crew who quickly moved away from the area. He then shouted and waved his arms at the presenters and they went up to the big man and shook his hand while the cameras started to roll.

The main presenter, a jolly man with a balding head, talked to the man for a few minutes then the suited man waved with an over-exaggerated movement to all the watching people and press and then climbed into the JCB and started the motor. Black smoke belched from the exhaust and then the machine settled into a steady thrum. He raised the bucket of the machine and manoeuvred the arm and bucket around in the air to get a feel of the machine but most people knew that he was just showing off. The town hall clock began to strike three when, with a cue from the programme director, he gave the arm one final flourish and dropped it, burying the bucket in the soft grass. Suddenly a massive bolt of lightning streaked and crackled down from the red-hued, heavily overcast sky and stuck the JCB throwing it up into the air like a toy. It crashed down with a loud thud and grating of metal into the soft earth the noise of which was immediately drowned out by an enormous crack of thunder which made everyone put their hands over their ears. All the onlookers were stunned. It was as if time had stood still. Everyone was petrified until a scream rang out and broke the spell. After that all hell erupted. Women screamed and fainted, children started crying, grown men fell to their knees in shock. Hugo's father spread his arms and wrapped them round his wife and son who were still in shock, the colour having drained completely from their faces.

Suddenly a voice came out of a megaphone. "Ladies and gentlemen please keep calm and leave the site as quickly as possible but please do not leave the area and assemble in the town hall car park as we would like to take down your details in case we need to contact you.

Those who were able started to leave, while those who had fainted or collapsed were being attended to by their friends and some first aid people who had been standing by. The Bennett family had just started to walk away when another terrific scream was heard but this time it was from next to the capsized JCB. A women wearing earphones and a Hi-Viz jacket with CREW on the back was standing next to the machine whose engine was still purring and pointing down at the ground. Some members of the crew and two special constables raced to where she was standing and then grabbed her and quickly turned her around. She buried her head in the shoulder of one of the other women who glanced at the scene and herself turned and was violently sick. The special police who were patrolling the event approached them and following a quick glance ushered them away as quickly as possible but even they were white-faced and ashen.

Lying under the overturned JCB could be seen the legs of a man wearing a smart grey suit. Nothing else could be seen of his body but since the JCB had buried itself at least a foot into the soft soil one could only surmise what state he was in. The man with the megaphone suddenly picked up his voice as someone whispered what had happened in his ear and he almost shouted in panic "Ladies and Gentlemen it is imperative that you leave the site immediately but please, I repeat, please do not leave the area. The police will need to take your details as there has been a tragic accident." Slowly the spectators dispersed and headed to the town hall car park which was being used as an emergency assembly point. Sirens could be heard in the distance as the emergency services raced to the site. After about ten minutes the site had been cleared except for the two specials who were standing next to the JCB in silence, looking very serious. On the other side of the green a thin stooped figure wrapped in a dirty old black cloak emerged from where he was hiding in a doorway observing the event. A quiet cackling chuckle could be heard momentarily over the now decreasing wind. The sky began to clear but the silence persisted giving the area a ghostly feel.

CHAPTER 11

The Rescue Plan

I t was quite late by the time the Bennett family returned to their home and slumped exhausted on the settee in the lounge all except Mrs Bennett who busied herself in the kitchen making a cup of tea and a snack since they had had nothing since their visit to the café earlier in the day. It had taken a long time for the police and authorities to process all the witnesses of the day's tragic events. Both Hugo and his father were very subdued. Mr Bennett switched on the TV to see if he could gather any further information about what had happened. Mrs Bennett brought in some sandwiches, some small cakes and three cups of tea. Not a word was said other than a mumbled "Thanks" from the settee.

"A tragic accident has occurred here in the heart of Bideford during the filming of that most popular programme Time Team" the reporter on the television was saying. "We have here the director of that programme who may be able to give us some more up to date information on what happened." The camera turned and the face of the director, who, with still ashen face, came into view. He explained had they had been asked by Dr Richard Benson, a distant relative of Sir Thomas Raymond, the infamous Judge who had lived, and died, in the house they were excavating if, as owner of the land, he might cut the first turf over the top of the house as a sort of symbol of its "resurrection". He had planned to rebuild the mansion to as close as he could to the original drawings, which he had discovered in the local archives. These drawings also indicated that the house had been originally built on the site of an old abbey and the Time Team presenters had been eager to excavate and explore any possible traces of this abbey before it was again covered by a building. Unfortunately the machine he was using to cut the turf was regrettably struck by a lightning bolt which overturned the vehicle and trapped him underneath, killing him.

The camera panned around showing the site and the JCB which had now been moved to recover the body and was upright but covered in mud...and what looked remarkably like blood. The programme went on to interview some more members of the public who had witnessed the accident including Mr Bennett who stood up extremely straight during the interview and spoke very authoritatively. He was followed by a senior police officer who must have polished his uniform especially and finally the lead presenter of the programme who showed no signs of his normal jovial, bubbly personality and was obviously still in a great state of shock. The subject of the programme suddenly changed to a politician talking about proposed changes to the benefit system. At this point Mr Bennett grabbed the TV remote and with the fading of the screen the room fell silent except for the munching of sandwiches and swallowing of tea. Finally Mr Bennett said "I think we've had enough excitement for today. I think it's time for bed." With that Mrs Bennett said with a grin on her face "who does that snobby person who was interviewed before the policeman think he is?" and with that picked up the dirty plates and cups, took them into the kitchen, and fitted them into the dishwasher. Mr Bennett blushed, coughed into his hand and the whole family made their way upstairs with a very subdued "Goodnight".

The next day Hugo lay in his bed pondering about the events of the day before and wondering if they had any connection with the tales Bird had told them, especially since yesterday had been the 25th of August. He could faintly hear noises from downstairs when his mother called up "Hugo! Emma's here." He had completely forgotten that she was coming again and he was about to shout out excitedly "OK coming." when he stopped himself and in a much more subdued tone shouted "OK Mum." after all she was only a girl and he did not want to seem too enthusiastic about meeting her especially as Stephanie was in the next room and would taunt him even more if he sounded too enthusiastic.

When he finally arrived downstairs Mrs Jones was in deep conversation with Hugo's mother while in front of them two mugs of tea steamed. Emma put down her mug of tea when Hugo came into the room and gave him a broad smile and a cheery "Hello." Hugo gave a sort of half smile and said "Hello." back but obviously trying to get some sympathy for witnessing yesterday's horrific events. It did not work on Emma. She gave a grimace that effectively said "well, be like that then." and picked up her mug of tea and went back to watching the programme that was showing on the TV in the kitchen. Hugo felt like an idiot and immediately regretted his attitude. He promised that he will try to make up for it later in that day. Mrs Jones finally got up to go. She kissed her daughter goodbye and after standing for what seemed an age at the doorstep, still talking to Hugo's mother, she finally got into her car and with the toot of her horn drove off to Bristol to collect her husband and Emma's dad.

"Well what are you two going to do today?" asked Mrs Bennett, as she busied herself around in the kitchen. "Oh, by the way Hugo, Emma will be staying over again tonight and possibly tomorrow. Mr Jones wanted to visit a friend of his in Gloucester and has been invited out to dinner with him and to some "old boys do" the next day. It might mean that they would get back very late and to save disturbing us and Emma they asked me if she could stay again. Since you seemed to have fun last time she stayed I said it would be alright. I haven't had time to change the sheets so Emma can use the spare room again. Is that OK with you Emma?" Mrs Bennett had just finished saying this when Stephanie came into the room and gave a sarcastic look at Hugo mouthing the word "girlfriend" at him but saying nothing within earshot of her mother. She spoke loudly, "Mum, when you go shopping will you get me some more deodorant I've run out." Hugo would have liked to mouth an obscenity at her but since his mouth was full of the last of the Sugar Puffs he just pushed his nose into the air and turned away. Emma answered for him, "We want to have another race on the computer. Hugo said he could beat me and I want to prove him wrong." "That's nice" replied his mother. "I hope you've tidied your room Hugo it was a complete mess the last time I looked in." "Yes Mum." Hugo replied knowing full well that he had done nothing and it was probably even more untidy than yesterday as he had just thrown his old clothes on the floor the night before as he was too upset to put them away. "Let's go play." announced Emma and with that Hugo took his now empty bowl over to the side of the kitchen and put it on the side of the sink. "In the dishwasher if you please" scolded his mother and then with a mumbled "Sorry" Emma and Hugo went up to his room.

"What a mess!" Emma exclaimed as she opened the door "it's even worse than it was before. I know. You tidy up a bit while I boot up the computer. After all if your mum comes up and it's not working then she will think something is up." "OK" replied Hugo but definitely showing a great lack of enthusiasm. It did not take long before Hugo had finished kicking his dirty clothes and finished-with toys under the bed so at least there was a clean space. Emma looked at him disapprovingly. "Your mother will kill you when she finds that lot." and pointed to the ends of the clothes left poking from under the bed. Hugo gave them one more kick and hunched his shoulders. "Now," Emma began, "tell me all about yesterday. I overheard some of what your mother was telling mine but she was whispering so that I could not hear, so quickly what really did happen?" Hugo went through the previous day especially emphasising the part where the lightning struck. "The JCB went flying up into the air and when it landed there was this horrible squish and blood spurted everywhere." He explained in graphic detail, throwing his arms into the air as he emphasised the "Squish"." Look" he said, and jumping to the floor he rummaged underneath his bed and pulled out the T shirt that he had worn the previous day. It had some spattering of mud on it but he said excitedly "Look! Look!" and he pointed to some small red splashes on the shirt that did look remarkably like splashes of blood. Emma held her hand up to her mouth as she inspected and then reinspected the shirt. Hugo then went on to explain in lurid detail all about how the police took all their names and addresses and how, they had told his father, that as he was one of the closest to the scene they may want to interview him later as a witness. As Emma gasped with shock and excitement Hugo threw the shirt back on the floor and kicked it under the bed.

From under the bed where Hugo had just kicked his shirt came a small but definite squeal or squeak, it was hard to determine which. The children looked at each other in surprise. "Did you hear something?" Emma asked. "It sounded like a mouse or something." Hugo replied. Emma suddenly pulled her feet onto the bed and held her knees as close to her chest as possible. Hugo kicked the shirt again and the noise was repeated. Hugo looked at Emma, who was now tucked as far as she could go into the corner, knees up to her eyes, then, he went on all fours and started to pull out the clothes from under his bed with his fingertips. He never realised how many clothes he had aggregated under his bed. Oh! And look, there was that missile that he had been looking for off his F16 model. As the extracted pile of clothes and debris accumulated behind Hugo he suddenly screamed and moved backwards banging his head on the underside of his bed. "What is it!" shouted Emma. "I don't know." Hugo replied with a trembling voice. "bbbut I think I saw something move. Emma gave a sort of squeak herself and pulled her knees even closer to her chest. Hugo suddenly went rigid and sort of whimpered. Then, still on all fours he slowly backed out from under his bed, eyes wide open but his face a ghostly white. "What is it? What is it? What is it?" Emma shrieked with panic in her voice. Hugo backed even further from the bed saying nothing but pointing to something emerging from the darkness from under where Emma was taking refuge. Both children wanted to scream but fear had made them both dumb. Slowly, a small figure about fifteen centimetres tall with a dirty, silver-coloured dress and fine gossamer wings emerged out of the darkness appearing to be as frightened as the two people in front of her.

"Wwwwho are you?" Hugo whispered as finally he found his voice. "I'm Puchy." The small figure replied, looking equally as terrified as the boy in front of her, "but you probably know me better as the Toothfairy." "The what?" Hugo almost screamed, leaning back and sitting on his haunches. "My name is Puchy and I'm the Toothfairy. I know you because I have already visited you a couple of times when you lost your other teeth and put them under your pillow. Normally you are not supposed to see me and that is why I always come when you are asleep but something has happened and I needed to talk to you." "What's happened?" said Emma who had unwrapped herself from her knees and was now hanging over the edge of the bed so that her head was upside down. The Toothfairy was taken aback at such a sight but then continued on. "I'm here because of Bird. He said you knew him. He has been captured by the wicked witch Kadavera and is being held prisoner in her cave. I managed to escape after Bird managed to free me but he was caught in the process and I think that the witch plans to kill him or use him in her terrible experiments. He asked me to come and see if you can help him escape." The Toothfairy sat down on the floor and began to cry. "I'm not supposed to let humans see me let alone talk to them but I didn't know what to do." "You did the right thing and we will certainly help you. Bird is our friend and there's nothing we won't do to help him." said Emma reassuringly "Right." agreed Hugo but with a little reluctance in his voice. "First of all." continued Emma "tell us all you know and then we can try and work out a plan." So the Toothfairy made herself comfortable and started to tell about how she was captured while trying to swap Hugo's tooth for some money, how she was taken to the witches cave and saw the experiments that the witch was doing and the poor animals that she used to test the potions out on. She went on to describe the layout of the cave and how finally Bird came to rescue her and the other animals but was captured himself in the process. She had just finished when she suddenly looked up and said. "Oh, and I forgot, Kadavera has got a funny looking cat that is very vicious but a bit of a coward but it has very good hearing. Hugo and Emma sat spellbound soaking in every word and when Puchy had finally stopped talking they both sat back in silence as they tried to formulate a plan to rescue Bird.

The silence was broken by Mrs Bennett calling up the stairs telling that their lunch was ready. "We have to go now for our lunch." Emma said apologetically. "If we don't then Hugo's Mother will think something is wrong." Hugo nodded in agreement and because all the excitement had made him feel very hungry. "We'll be back shortly." Emma went on. "If we want you how do we get hold of you or do fairies have mobiles too." Emma and Hugo grinned at the thought of a fairy with a mobile phone. "Call my name three times. Remember it's, Puchy, and I will come to you." The Toothfairy replied and with that the children started to go down to the kitchen for their lunch but just before closing the bedroom door Emma turned back and asked Puchy if there was anything she could get her for her lunch. "If you can get me some sugar?" She said "that would be very nice. I normally drink nectar from flowers but I know that you don't have that so some sugar will do." The two closed the door and went downstairs.

"You've been very quiet up there?" Mrs Bennett said as they entered the kitchen. "How's the game?" "We've been doing some puzzles from a book that I found on my shelf." lied Hugo and without any further conversation they tucked into their lunches. The food did not last long as they were both eager to get back and formulate a plan with Puchy to rescue Bird. Hugo had already thought out that they will need to go back to the cave to elicit a rescue, so, to pre-empt some awkward questions from his parents, Hugo asked his mother if they could have another picnic along the railway track as they had enjoyed it so much the other day. A thought suddenly crossed Hugo's mind. Last time they went they took Jake but if they took him this time his boisterousness and barking would make it impossible to keep up any level of stealth and so Hugo announced, almost as a statement rather than a request. "We can't take Jake this time because last time he broke into a farmer's field and started to chase the sheep and the farmer said that if he saw the dog again he'd shoot it." Emma looked at him questioningly but slowly the penny dropped and she smiled and nodded her head. "Well that was very wrong of the farmer to say that to such young children but I understand what he meant and you should have looked after Jake a little better. In that case Jake can come shopping with me." Emma nodded her head again and they left the table and returned upstairs to the bedroom and Puchy to plan, not forgetting to pilfer a big handful of sugar from under Mrs Bennett's nose

When they entered the bedroom Hugo was absolutely amazed to see that his room was tidy, spotless even. The clothes from under the bed had been dragged out and neatly folded. The toys had been put back on the shelf or in the toy cupboard. The broken ones had even been repaired. The crooked pictures on his walls were straight and those posters that were peeling off the walls had been reattached with Blutac. Hugo just stood there with his mouth open. He could not believe it. The room had never looked so spick and span. Even when his mother became so frustrated with the mess that she went in and tidied it the room had never looked so good. "He flopped on the bed and said "Blimey! What's happened.!" Just then Puchy came into view and said, wiping her face and flicking the dust off her wings. "I thought that gnomes were messy but humans must come a close second." Emma burst out laughing while Hugo still sat there, mouth gaping and looking a little embarrassed. "However will I explain this to Mum?" he mumbled. "Never mind that. Let's get down to business." Emma said authoritatively but it took several minutes before Hugo had recovered and could set his mind to thinking up a plan to rescue Bird.

"Firstly we need to know the exact layout of the cave." He began. He had seen a programme on the television where the goodies had had a similar problem after one of their number had been captured by the baddies and so he wracked his brain to think of what they had done but all he could remember was them starting by getting a plan of the baddies cave, or was it a castle, he couldn't quite remember. Nevertheless, Emma retrieved a note book and pencil from the now tidy desk and under the directions of the Toothfairy she drew a rough sketch of the layout of the witches cave and placed a big X in the spot where Puchy thought that Bird may be being kept. "We'll need something to make the entrance bigger so that we can get inside and a torch because it is very dark." said Hugo. "I know I'll pop down into the garage and see what dad's got in his tool box." And with that eased himself off the bed, stretched and went downstairs to the garage to search amongst his father's tools. Minutes later he burst back into the room holding his chest. From underneath his shirt he pulled a small hammer with a claw end, a large screw driver and a big black torch which he flashed at Emma and Puchy to show them it worked. "Excellent." said Emma excitedly "but look at the time there isn't enough time to get to the entrance of the cave let alone get in and rescue Bird. I'm sorry Puchy but I know that your extremely concerned about Bird, so are we, but if we go now, goodness knows what time we would get back and Hugo's parents would be very worried and would find it very hard to explain my being away to my parents. What we'll do is get up very early tomorrow and make an early start so that should give us plenty of time." Puchy looked a little downcast but agreed that Emma had a point but then she suddenly looked up and said "I know. I'll go and see if the gnomes will help. They may have some ideas. I know that they are a bit grumpy and hate doing anything for anyone else unless there's something in it for them but it's worth a try." With that she jumped onto the window sill, waved, shouted "See you tomorrow." and with a flicker of her almost transparent wings she disappeared. "Let's go down and ask mum if she can make us another picnic for tomorrow and tell her that we want to leave as early as possible so that we don't arrive home late like last time?" "Good idea." Responded Emma and they both rose from the bed and went downstairs.

"What have you been up to?" asked Mrs Bennett as they walked into the lounge. She lowered the magazine she was reading to look at them. "We've been sorting out my room?" Hugo replied with an ear to ear smile on his face. He looked at Emma who also smiled but more at Hugo's audacity to take the credit for something he had nothing to do with. "Well that's good." said Mrs Bennett but under her breath she muttered "I'll believe that when I see it." "I bet you two are feeling hungry. I've made a small snack for now, help yourself to drinks out of the fridge. We'll have dinner properly when your father gets back. He's had to go to the police station to give a full statement on that awful accident yesterday. I don't know how long he'll be but I'm sure it won't be long.

Hugo and Emma started to tuck into the sandwiches and buns that Hugo's mother had set out. While he was eating, Hugo asked his mother if they could leave early the next day and would she make a picnic like the other day. Mrs Bennett was a little surprised at the request as "getting up early" was not in Hugo's vocabulary but she smiled and said that she would since they had gone to the trouble of tidying Hugo's room, which she still not believe. Hugo's father did not get in till late and when he did arrive he suggested all going out to a small restaurant that had just opened in the centre of Westward Ho! He said that it was far too late for them to cook a proper dinner and it would be very pleasant to eat out for a change and support local trade. So everyone, including Stephanie, who was looking miserable because she and Marty had had words and had separated unharmoniously. It was late when they all returned and Hugo and Emma went to their rooms and were soon fast asleep.

CHAPTER 12

The Gnomes

Puchy was very used to traveling in the dark for that is what it was by the time she reached the Gnome Reserve. The gnomes were all active at this time as there were no humans about to observe them. She could see them all about wheeling their barrows, digging the soil, planting vegetables and the such like. Many had taken off their brightly coloured coats and pointed red hats and were working in their shirt sleeves. They all gave her a cheery wave as she passed them. She thought that her best chance of getting help would be to find Barguff. As he had already been captured and knew how bad Kadavera really was. If anyone was going to help it would be him.

She found him sitting beside a large pond. He had a long fishing rod in his hands and was gazing intently at a large red round float that was bobbing on the surface of the water. As she approached him he gave a loud "Shuuuuuuuuuuush!" but then suddenly jumped up and stamped his foot firmly on the ground. "You silly creature, you've made me miss him. I've been after that goldfish for weeks and I just had him on the line and you scared him off. What do you want anyway?"

The Toothfairy apologised profusely for scaring off Barguff's fish adding that he could always try again tomorrow. This made the irate gnome even angrier. "I wanted him today not tomorrow you silly imp." "I'm not an imp, I'm a fairy." The Toothfairy" retorted "and if you must know and I'm here to ask your help to free Bird from that wicked witch Kadavera." The name of the witch suddenly made the gnome stop ranting and become quiet. Puchy explained to him how Bird had rescued her but in the process had been captured himself. She then went on to tell him how two humans were going to help as well and they were going the next day to try to rescue their friend. Barguff paid close attention but when he heard that two humans were involved he suddenly straightened and said "Sorry can't help you. We gnomes can't expose ourselves to humans even if their intentions are good." And with that he picked up his rod and fishing basket and started walking briskly down the path towards a small pink cottage with diamond-glazed windows and a straw-thatched roof. Puchy chased after him begging and pleading with him to change his mind but when he arrived at the cottage he opened the door, went in and slammed it behind him. Several other gnomes had seen and heard her pleading but they too gave her a wide berth. She sat on the cottage step sobbing and despite several calls through the red-painted letter box, the gnome stayed silent. At last she realised that there was absolutely no further point in trying and with a loud sniff flew off to rest before the big day tomorrow with her real friends.

CHAPTER 13

Into the Witches Cave

Hugo woke with banging on his door "Come on! Time to get up. We've got a lot to do today." He recognised Emma's voice but it took him a few moments to realise what was happening. Then it all came flooding back to him and he got, or fell, out of bed and rushed to open his door. Emma was standing there fully dressed with a pair of denim jeans and a white T shirt with a large pink picture of Barbie emblazoned over the front. On her head she wore a towel which she was rubbing around to try to dry her hair. "Come on, I've already had a shower and your mother has finished cooking breakfast, bacon and eggs with fried bread followed by toast. Hugo rushed back inside, threw on his clothes, started to head for the bathroom to clean his teeth then thought, "Oh fiddlesticks, I haven't got time. I'm sure dad will understand." but he said that with his fingers crossed, turned and rushed downstairs.

The whole family were already seated around the kitchen table tucking into their breakfasts. Mr Bennett looked up and said "Come on sleepyhead. I thought that you wanted to make an early start?" He smiled and then went back to his egg and bacon and reading his newspaper which took up half the breakfast table. "I see we've made the national newspapers with all the happenings at the Time Team escapade. "Hey look!" he went on excitedly "There's a bit here that says, "one of the witnesses, Dr Paul Bennett, a local dentist, who was at the front of the spectators said" that it was the worst thing he had ever seen and something he would never forget. He would like to extend his sympathy for the relatives of the deceased on their tragic loss." He sat back and smiled at his wife. "Well I suppose that's my fifteen minutes of fame over with." Mrs Bennett grinned and went back to putting out Hugo's breakfast plate. There was a general buzz of conversation about the incident and the fact that Mr Bennett had been mentioned in the Daily Telegraph for the next ten minutes until finally breakfast was finished. Hugo's father folded the newspaper popped it into his briefcase, kissed his wife on the cheek and left for work, still smiling to himself.

Hugo and Emma both went up to their rooms to finish getting ready. Hugo decided to clean his teeth after all, in case his dad found out. At last they were ready to go. His mother told him that she had prepared some food for them both and packed it into his rucksack with some drinks. Hugo strapped it onto his back and then suddenly said, "Oh! Hang on a minute, I've forgotten something." And turning he stormed back up the stairs to his bedroom. Emma tapped her foot and looked at her watch. With a great scramble Hugo came down the stairs two at a time and joined Emma who gave him an annoyed look. When they finally started along the old railway track Hugo apologised and explained that he had forgotten to pack the tools and torch as he had hidden them in his room just in case his mother spotted them when she was packing the rucksack. "Good thinking." Emma commented and her mood improved.

They were about half way along the track to the cave entrance when Emma suddenly stopped and said "What about Puchy? We've forgotten about her." "Who!" queried Hugo, then suddenly realised who she meant. "Let's try calling her." Emma suggested and called out "Puchy, Puchy, Puchy. Where are you?" but nothing happened. Emma called again but there was no sign of the small Toothfairy. "We'll try again later." said Hugo and they resumed their march along the track but now looking left and right to see if they could see any sign of their fairy friend. Eventually, a little out of breath as they had set quite a fast walking pace, they reached the cave entrance, still marked by the cairn of white stones. Sitting on the top of one of the stones was Puchy. She looked very sad but on seeing Hugo and Emma she immediately brightened up and wiggled her wings. "I heard you call me she said but since I was already here I thought it best if I wait for you to arrive." Hugo had already unfastened the rucksack and had his head buried in it retrieving the tools and torch, which he laid out onto the ground with a look of satisfaction on his face. "I'll get to work then." He said but not before looking around to ensure that they were not being observed. Taking up the hammer and screwdriver he started to break away the earth and rocks that surrounded the entrance to the cave but in as quiet a manner as he could.

It took about half an hour to widen the hole to make it big enough to crawl through by which time Hugo was sweating quite profusely. Emma had asked, while Hugo was digging, "If the hole is this small how does what's her name Kada something get in an out?" "It's Kadavera, and she can turn herself into a sort of vapour so that she can get through even the smallest holes." replied Puchy. "Done it!" Hugo finally exclaimed and wiped his forehead with his sleeve. He put the tools back into the rucksack, took out a bottle of juice, had a big mouthful straight out of the bottle, Emma gave him a disgusted look, and lifted the now lit torch above his head. She waved it and said. "Well then what are we waiting for but remember be absolutely silent. We don't know what we will find when we get there and I don't know about you two but I have no desire to come face to face with what's her name." With that all three squeezed through the opening and stealthily crept down the long tunnel that led to the cave and the hopeful rescue of their friend.

The three friends moved slowly down the tunnel straining their eyes through the gloom. Hugo took the torch from Emma since "as a man he should be in the lead." At this she gave him a black look and said sarcastically "Well take it then, leader." He did not notice the sarcasm in her voice but carefully took the torch. He put his hand over the front of it so that only the minimum of light was emitted, just enough to see where they were going. Hugo did not want to reveal his presence from the light of the torch. They had all been going for several minutes when Hugo stopped and switched off the torch. He squinted his eyes as he desperately tried to peer through the darkness at the small flickering light several hundred yards ahead of him. Water dripped from the small white stalactites that covered the roof. Slowing the pace the three moved closer and closer to the rotting door marking the entrance to the cave. A beam of flickering light flashed from a hole near the base of the door. "This must have been how Barguff managed to escape." thought Puchy. Hugo approached the door and put his ear to it. Silence, except for the occasional crackling of a fire. Puchy flew down to the ground and looked through the hole in the door. Nothing stirred.

Slowly Hugo put his weight against the door and with a low creaking it gave and started to open. Hugo was concerned that the hinges would squeal and give the game away. He remembered seeing a programme on the television where a detective was hunting a criminal and so he tried to copy what he had seen. In the programme the squeaking hinges had given the detective away so he did not want to make the same mistake. Luckily, fortune was with them and the door slowly and silently moved open. As carefully as he could Hugo peered around the door. Emma pushed him so that she could get a better look and Hugo nearly tumbled forwards. He turned on her and was about to give her a telling off when she put her finger to her lips and he suddenly remembered to be quiet.

All three inched around the cave with their backs against the walls, their eyes darting left and right trying to make out the features of the cavern but more especially for any sign of the witch or her companion Snatch. They had progressed almost half way round the cave when Emma spotted some wooden boxes stacked in a dark recess. She pointed at them to Hugo who nodded and slowly made his way over to them. Sure enough, by peering through the slats of the box he saw the distinctive purple colour of the stripe that ran down Bird's back. The other two joined him. He poked his finger between the planks and touched Bird's back. Bird fluffed his feathers but did not respond. He poked him harder but again no positive response. He poked him again, even harder and at the same time whispered. "Bird, Bird, It's us." Bird's head snapped round and moved to look through the holes in the crate in which he was being held. "What in the world are you doing here?" he said and then realised that he was almost shouting and so dropped his voice and repeated "What in the world are you doing here?"

"Yes! What in the world are you doing here?" cackled a loud voice from behind them and before they knew it they had all been covered by a thick heavy net from which there was no escape. "Very nice of you all to drop in and visit poor old Kadavera. We don't get many guests do we Snatch." The cold voice continued. "Friends of yours are they my fine feathered friend. I am sure you are all very welcome and at such an opportune moment. I have some really new potions for you to try out. I'm sure that you'll find them absolutely delicious. By the way, I may not have very good eyesight after those wretched crows attacked me but my sense of smell is perfect and you my pretty young thing" she gazed down at Emma," do smell so fragrantly. I could smell you coming the moment you entered my tunnel." Hugo looked at Emma and sniffed. Sure enough she did smell. What on earth have you got on?" Hugo choked. Emma's face turned bright red and she looked down at the ground. "Well while I was getting ready this morning Stephanie said I could try on some of the new deodorant that your mother bought her yesterday and I must have put too much on. I'm sorry. I'm really sorry." And with that she started to cry. Hugo sighed "Women." then, taking her hand he said "It's too late now, never mind. What are we going to do?" "You're going to DIE!" screamed the witch and turned away laughing hysterically. Emma's crying grew louder and was joined by that of Puchy. "Look after our guests Snatch, while I find them some comfortable homes to live in...for now!" the last two words the witch spat out. The weird looking cat-like creature snarled and then prowled up and down never taking its eyes off the new "guests". Bird moved around inside his box so that he now face all three dejected characters. He looked at Puchy and admonished her saying "I told you NOT to get these two involved. Now it's going to be even harder to escape." Puchy redoubled her crying and truth be known, Hugo was fighting away the tears as well.

The witch quickly returned dragging three wooden crates behind her, two largish ones and a small one. Emma and Hugo were thrown into each of the large boxes and Puchy into the small one. With a sigh of triumph Kadavera hammered down the lids. Turning, she headed back to the recesses of her cave, Snatch, still growling and spitting following on behind. The laughing cackle could still be heard for several minutes until all again was silent. Emma and Puchy slowly regained their composure and other than the occasional sniff, began to settle down. "What are we going to do now?" asked Emma between sniffs. "All of us are trapped and no one even knows where we are." "I'm sure we can think of something." Bird said reassuringly but even he was at a loss on how they were going to get away.

CHAPTER 14

Rescued

All four lay huddled in their respective boxes thinking of ways they could escape the future that Kadavera was, at this very moment, planning for them all and contemplating the things that they would like to do to her, if and when, they did finally escape. No words were spoken as each searched deep into their thoughts for a solution. All that could be heard was the incessant drip of the water from the roof into the puddles on the floor. Over half an hour went by. All noise had ceased from the part of the cave to where Kadavera and Snatch had gone.

There was a little tap on the side of Birds crate followed by another. Bird, roused from his thoughts turned to see what was causing the tapping. Squinting through the boards of his box he could make out a small figure dressed in a blue coat, yellow trousers and a bright red pointed hat. "Barguff." Bird almost choked. "Is that you? What are you doing here?" "Trying to save you lot." He said gruffly. "You really have got yourself into a right mess this time and dragged these "Humans", he almost spat out the word, into it as well. You should be ashamed of yourself."

The whispering from Birds crate made the other three prisoners stir and turn around. Did I say three, I should have said four, for lying in a box adjacent to Bird's was the pathetic body of Thwack the rabbit who Kadavera had used for her trials on her daylight potion. He was not dead but was certainly the worse for his experiences and time in captivity. Hugo, Emma and Puchy were all shocked to see the little man and were about to cry out in surprise but Bird made a whispered "Shuuush," however, Puchy wiggled around in her box and whispered "You came Barguff, you came. Thank you. Thank you. Thank you." Barguff blushed but thankfully it could not be seen in the gloom. "Well I got to thinking that you might need a bit of help so, since I knew where the cave was, I decided to come and see if I was right and obviously I was." He said with great satisfaction. "Right Barguff, enough talking get us out of here." implored Bird "and be quick about it before old wrinkle-features comes back again. Hugo and Emma smiled. Bird had obviously not lost his sense of humour.

Barguff pushed and pulled at the lid of Birds crate but to no avail, he was just not strong enough. "If you free me first" spouted Puchy "my box is the smallest and most frail and then when I am free we can both open Hugo's and Emma's, I mean the human's, boxes and then we can all try to open Birds." "You're quite bright for a fairy." responded Barguff. "I was just about to suggest that myself." Hugo and Emma looked at each other and smiled. Baguff made short shrift of opening Puchy's box and she flew out and started to help Barguff prise open the lid of the one containing Hugo. This one was a little more difficult but with a final creak the top gave way Hugo stood up and stretched. He rapidly hopped out and then all three quickly opened and freed Emma from her temporary prison. Now all four pushed and heaved on the lid of Birds container but it would not budge. "If only I still had my tools in my rucksack." wished Hugo. Then suddenly he slapped his forehead as he quietly exclaimed "How stupid I am." and with that he dug deep into his trouser pocket and after much rummaging around he proudly pulled out a small penknife with a red handle and a silver cross embedded in it. "He held the knife above his head, waving it and showing it to everyone with a look of absolute delight on his face. He opened the knife in the section with the screwdriver blade and using it he was quickly able to dislodge the nails holding the lid and with a fluffing and flurry of feathers Bird was free.

"Right then, let's get out of here." Bird said and they all turned to leave but there was a noise behind them and a faint voice said "Please take me with you?" "Thwack. It's Thwack." cried Puchy. "Please we must save his as well." Rapidly Hugo took out his penknife again and with a few short flicks the poor rabbit was freed. "Thank you." it squawked. Bird immediately saw that the rabbit was worse for wear and might slow down their escape so he instructed Hugo to put the poor animal on his back and he would carry him to safety. With this done, all six escapees started to move around the outside of the cave wall. "Wait a minute." Hugo cried and he bent down at a nearby puddle of water and started to splash it all over Emma. "What in the world are you playing at?" she whispered scornfully and fought to stop him doing it. But he mouthed the word "Deodorant." and she suddenly understood why. She also then started to splash as much water over herself as possible to eliminate her "Smell". They continued on until they came to the door, which thankfully was still open. They all went through when Hugo suddenly stopped and turned. He rummaged again in the depths of his trouser pockets and finally pulled out a length of string. "I thought that this might come in useful for something." he said and quietly closing the cave door he tied the string around the handle and a large rock that was jutting out from the side of the wall. "That might give us a bit more time." He quietly said and still slowly they all inched their way, in the darkness, back up the tunnel.

They could all now see the light at the entrance to the tunnel and picked up the pace. The air was beginning to become sweeter and everyone, even poor old Thwack was feeling that freedom was at hand when the tunnel echoed to a blood curdling scream and the words "No! No! No! That's impossible." All six suddenly rushed for the entrance. They heard another loud squeal but this time from Snatch and the sound of a heavy thud as Kadavera kicked him and screamed "Out of my way you stupid animal."

Hugo, Emma, Bird, Puchy, Barguff and Thwack stumbled out of the cave and into bright sunlight. They all fell onto the grass panting. The noise of the crashing waves on the rocks below and the occasional cry of a seagull above confirmed to every one of them that they were safe. Thwack coughed and quietly spoke. "You must all get away from here immediately. Kadavera can now exist in daylight. The potion she tried out on me worked. If you don't get away now she will come after us and we will end up as prisoners again but it was too late. With an almighty rush of noise and foul air Kadavera swooshed through the tunnel entrance and stopped, facing and towering over the recumbent escapees. "Thought you could get the better of me, did you?" she chortled. "Well, you didn't and this time I'm not going to make any mistakes." With this she raised a long knife above her head and moved toward Bird. "You first." she hissed.

Just at that point Thwack started to cough violently and appeared to be having convulsions on the ground. He suddenly went rigid and then relaxed. He looked into Kadavera's eyes and started to laugh interspersed by coughing. "I think the last laugh is on you, you stupid old hag. You see your potion wasn't perfect and it's wearing off. The sunlight is killing me and it's going to kill you too." He gave a final cough and lay motionless on the grass, a beam of sunlight poking through the clouds, illuminating his body.

Kadavera stopped in her tracks. "That's impossible. It was perfect. I made sure it was perfect." She slowly lowered her arm. The knife dropped from her hand which went to her throat. She started to cough violently and fell to the floor. "Help me. Help me. Please help me" she gasped but no one moved, petrified by the sight in front of them. The dying witch writhed on the ground as the sunbeam slowly moved from Thwack to her. A violent scream of "NO!" rent the air and the body slumped to the ground and lay motionless.

All six did not, could not, move. They all stood there in stunned silence. Suddenly the black cloak of the witch began to move and shimmer. It became as if vapourising into smoke and slowly transformed into the body of a beautiful young girl, dressed in a flowing white dress but with a deep red scare cut into her neck around which hung a fine necklace which in turn supported a gold locket with a brilliant green stone. On her finger she wore a large gold ring also sporting a brilliant green stone mounted in it. They image shimmered and moved till it was caught by a slight breeze and slowly it disintegrated and disappeared into the ether. All that was left, lying between two small stones with funny zig-zag patterns on them, was the necklace and the ring which glinted and shone in the afternoon sunlight.

Hugo was the first to move. Everyone was stunned at what they had witnessed and it took several minutes for them to recover. Emma had started to cry and Puchy followed soon after. Hugo went forward and gingerly picked up the locket and ring. He carefully examined both and seeing that the locket could open he tried to prise it apart but the two halves fitted tightly. He also noticed on the front of the locket was engraved a large letter "M" in an elaborate script. Holding both pieces in one hand he sought again in his pocket and finding it, withdrew his penknife. He opened the small blade and used it to finally open the two halves of the locket. Inside he saw two small miniature paintings. On one side was a picture of two very beautiful young women, one of which looked exactly like that of the apparition he had just seen. The other painting was of a young man and a young girl, both smiling and looking very happy. He turned and showed the locket to everyone else who each in turn took it and gasped at the beauty of the women in the pictures and how happy they all looked. Similarly, Hugo passed round the ring and again they were all shocked to see how it sparkled and shone in the sunlight. "Where's Thwack?" Puchy suddenly cried out having now come out of her stupor and looking around. "He evaporated, just like the witch." Barguff wheezed "but there's nothing left of him." Puchy began to cry again, "I really liked Thwack. "she sobbed. "we got to be quite good friends while were trapped in the cave. I shall miss him. I really will." "So will we all." cut in Emma "We all liked him too." With that she went up to the tiny fairy and wrapped a couple of fingers around her to give her a reassuring cuddle as best she could.

"Those items you've got there could be very well cursed." Bird said to Hugo "and I think it would be best if you got rid of them." Hugo looked at the necklace, locket and ring and then back at Bird. "I'll think about it." He replied and with that he put everything into his trouser pocket. "Look at the time Hugo!" screamed Emma "If we don't leave immediately we'll be late again and your mum will go mad." "Rrright " said Hugo and turned to face Bird, Puchy and Barguff. "I really have enjoyed meeting you all." He stammered and thanks for coming to our aid Barguff. I really don't know what we would have done without you." Barguff blushed. This time everyone could see him. "Oh it was nothing. Glad I could be of service. Anytime you need my help just call me…. Three times that is but don't ever tell any of the other gnomes that I helped a human. I will never hear the last of it." "Same goes for me" replied Bird. "And me." squeaked Puchy. "See you all again soon." Shouted Hugo and with Emma, together they turned and started to walk briskly away. They turned back to wave goodbye but no one could be seen.

"How's your day been? You're just in time for tea." Mrs Bennett asked as Emma and Hugo came into the house. "Not too bad" said Hugo unenthusiastically. "I lost my rucksack. It slid off a rock we were sitting on while we were having our picnic and fell down a deep hole" Hugo smiled and winked at Emma. "And it was too deep for me to reach to get it back." "Well as long as you didn't get into trouble trying to get it back then that's OK." Hugo blushed and turned his head away so that his mother did not see him. Tea was eaten in relative silence until the doorbell rang and Emma's mother and father were at the door. Emma put down the cake she was eating and ran to the door. Her father picked her up in his arms and gave her a big kiss. "Did you miss me." he said and Emma hugged him round the neck and gave him a big kiss. All of them sat down at the kitchen table and talked about everything with special emphasis on the Time Team Incident but strangely there was no mention of Birds, fairies, gnomes or witches, not even rabbits. Eventually, the Jones's got up to leave. Mr and Mrs Jones thanked Hugo's mother for looking after Emma and Emma reiterated the comment. "I bet you two will be glad to get back to school next week?" said Mr Jones. Hugo had quite forgotten that the school holidays were nearly over. "Spoze so." Hugo replied, deliberately trying to sound unenthusiastic. He looked at Emma and they smiled at each other. The Jones's gave a final farewell, got in their car and with a toot on the horn they drove off.

Hugo settled into the lounge and watched some programmes on the television. He didn't pay them much attention as his mind was still back at the cave. Eventually it was time for bed and it was not long before he fell fast asleep. In the morning he woke to find the weather outside had turned and it was pouring with rain. He wasn't sure if the adventure of the previous day was for real or was it a dream or had he imagined it. Well his room was still tidy, at least that part was true but it wasn't until he was straightening his pillow that he caught sight of a small flash of light. He pulled back his pillow and there in the very centre was a sparkling, brand-new two pound coin and beside it a small piece of pink paper on which was written in small handwriting "Thank You. Puchy". Hugo laughed out loud. Tossed the coin into the air and went downstairs for breakfast. Look what the Toothfairy left me he said to his parents, again tossing the coin high into the air and catching it. "Oh very nice." His father said but looking at his wife he looked puzzled and hunched his shoulders. She looked back equally perplexed. Hugo tossed the coin once more into the air and then pushed it into his pocket. He suddenly froze. His hand came to rest on the ring and necklace that had belonged to Kadavera and the words of Bird suddenly came back to him. "Those items you've got there could very well be cursed."

CHAPTER 15

The White Stones

Hugo had finished his breakfast and was sat on his bed with the ring in one hand and the locket and necklace in the other. They were such beautiful objects that he really wanted to keep them but he kept on remembering Bird's warning. "I know what I can do" he said to himself, straightening up. "I'll hide them so that in reality I don't have them but if I ever need them I will know where to find them." With this decision his mood lightened and he tried to think of a suitable hiding place. He thought for over an hour even walking all around every room in the house, well except for Stephanie's and his parents' bedrooms. He was sat on the back doorstep throwing pebbles at an old bucket when he had a brilliant idea. Why had he not thought of that in the first place?

In the afternoon the rain stopped but it stayed overcast. Hugo put on his jacket and said to his mother that he was going to take Jake for a walk. At the word "Walk" Jake jumped up and started barking and wagging his tail frantically. "I'm sure that that dog can understand English" she said to no one in particular. "Don't be too late Hugo." She shouted after him as Hugo led Jake out of the house and back down the old railway track. Jake had been cooped up in the house all morning as Mrs Bennett did not want to let him out in the rain as he would make such a mess when he came back in and she had just washed the kitchen floor. Hugo unlatched Jake's lead and he ran up and down the track enjoying the freedom. Eventually they reached the site of the entrance to the witches cave. All was as it had been when Hugo and Emma had left. The small cairn of white quartz stones was still there were Hugo had built it several days earlier. Hugo dug in his pocket and pulled out the necklace on which hung the locket and the bright green ring. He played with them in his hands. He again prised open the locket with his penknife and gazed at the picture of the three beautiful women and the handsome young man inside. Eventually he snapped the locket shut and moving some of the white stones he buried the treasures deep in the centre of the cairn. He restored the stones back to their original places, dusted his hands and wiped them in his trousers. He turned and went back home with Jake bouncing along beside him. He looked back several times wondering if he had done the right thing but he eventually reassured himself that he had and marched on.

Hugo had just rounded a bend in the track which meant that he could no longer see the cairn when a dark figure approached the cairn. A long thin scrawny hand emerged from beneath the tattered cloak and started to move the stones. A glint revealed the hand had on its ring finger a large gold ring with a sparkling blue stone. The hand grasped the ring, necklace and locket from beneath the stones and then the figure seemed to evaporate leaving no trace.

THE END?

Lightning Source UK Ltd.
Milton Keynes UK
UKOW04f0714180215

246470UK00003B/208/P